"Brimming with charm and philosophical humor, *The Skunks* sweeps readers into a young woman's first foray into adulthood. This is a novel that asks big questions of friendship, romantic firsts, and finding one's way in the world. Prepare to be dazzled—Fiona Warnick is a wunderkind."

—Allegra Hyde,
author of *The Last Catastrophe*

"*The Skunks* is a gleaming, zany little gem—a novel that perfectly captures the weirdness of being young and just out of college, and not sure what comes next. Compassionate, quirky, and beautifully written, I adored it."

—Annie Hartnett,
author of *Rabbit Cake* and *Unlikely Animals*

"One summer can change everything in *The Skunks*. A relatable and heartwarming capture of that pivotal coming-of-age moment in early adulthood when the world is demanding you make declarations about who you are, but you aren't quite sure yet. Warnick gets at the pangs of awkward encounters, the trials of returning to your hometown, and most of all, finding love within yourself. An inventive new novel that ensures you'll never think of skunks the same way. A joy to read."

—Chelsea Bieker,
' ⸺ of *Godshot* and *Heartbroke*

T0281937

"A sly, graceful ode to the natural world, to the gray areas of human relationships, to love, to friendship, and to stories, *The Skunks* captivated me from the first page and kept on surprising me til the very end."

—**Jenny Fran Davis**,
author of *Dykette*

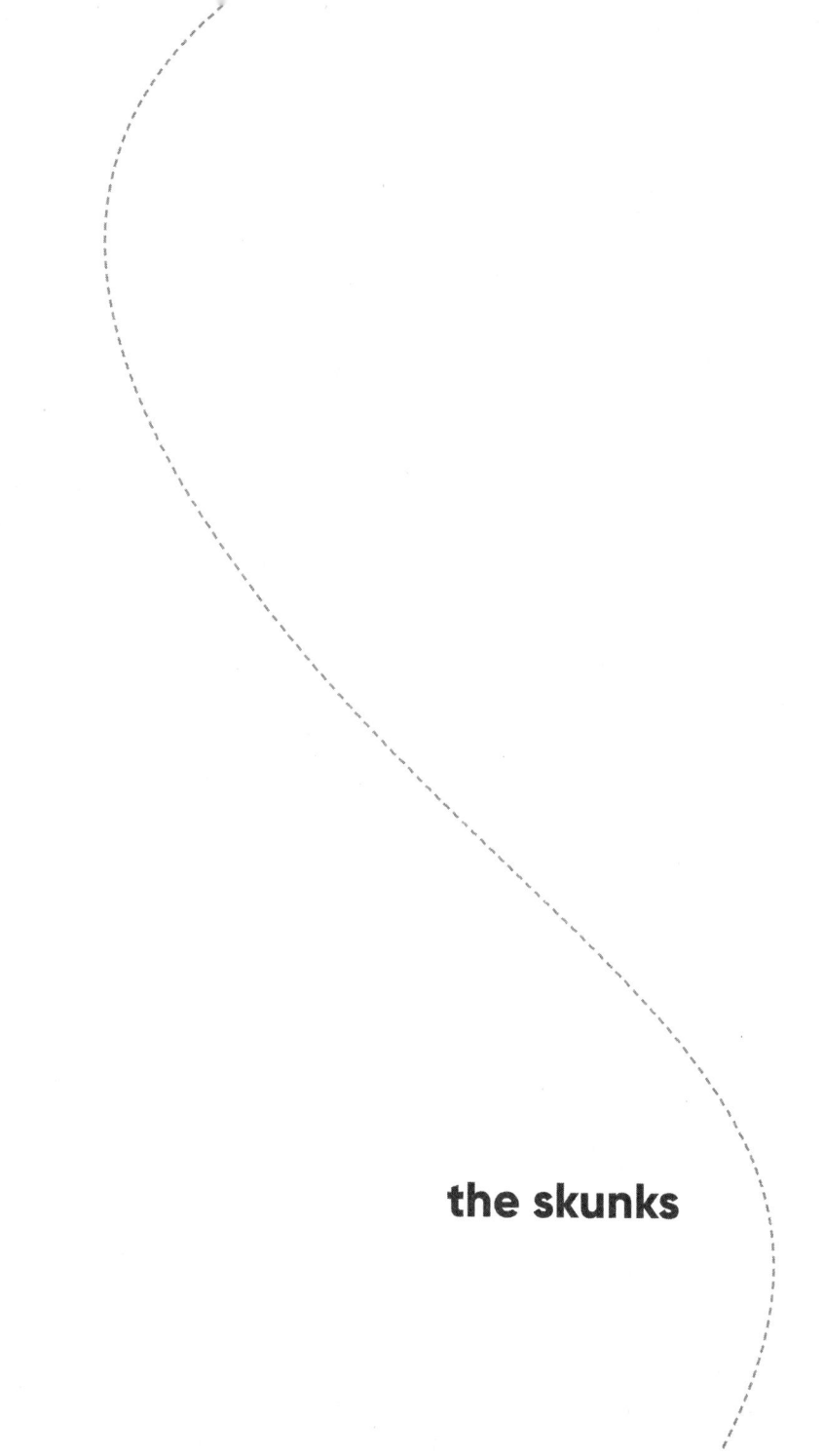

the skunks

the
skunks

a novel

fiona
warnick

Tin House
Portland, Oregon

First US Edition 2024
Printed in the United States of America

Manufacturing by Sheridan
Interior design by Beth Steidle

Library of Congress Cataloging-in-Publication Data

Names: Warnick, Fiona, 1999– author.
Title: The skunks : a novel / Fiona Warnick.
Description: First US edition. | Portland, Oregon : Tin House, 2024.
Identifiers: LCCN 2024000286 | ISBN 9781959030614 (paperback) |
ISBN 9781959030676 (ebook)
Subjects: LCGFT: Bildungsromans. | Novels.
Classification: LCC PS3623.A86427 S58 2024 |
DDC 813/.6—dc23/eng/20240109
LC record available at https://lccn.loc.gov/2024000286

TIN HOUSE
2617 NW Thurman Street, Portland, OR 97210
www.tinhouse.com

Distributed by W. W. Norton & Company

1 2 3 4 5 6 7 8 9 0

for Western Massachusetts

the skunks

june

Once upon a time there were three skunks.

What is the tense for the things that have happened and continue to happen? The moon orbits. A child fails to tell its mother it loves her as often as it should. The universe expands, without edges or observers.

There were three skunks, and they walk perpetually across the lawn.

The first time I saw the skunks, it was a Wednesday morning. I was taking the trash out. The sun was up, but the pavement under my bare feet was cold from the night.

I'd almost forgotten to take the trash out. The carrot end was what reminded me. Once, I'd had a crush on a boy who liked to put fried eggs over piles of raw grated carrot. You could put sauce on it if you wanted, he said, but the texture was the important part. The boy lived in Seattle now. I'd been trying to elevate my breakfast, and to give myself a reason to text him.

Look, the text would say, *I tried your recipe!*

And there would be a photo of a perfectly fried egg on top of a pile of grated carrots.

I gathered materials: the egg, the carrot, the frying pan. It took me a while to find the box grater. It was in the cabinet with the Tupperware. I grated the carrot until I couldn't grate anymore without grating the pads of my fingers. Then I held the leftover carrot nubbin over the trash. Then I remembered Jan and Steve had a compost pile. Then I remembered it was trash day.

It was a relief to remember, though it didn't matter in any material sense if I forgot. I hadn't produced much waste. But to forget would have marked my first week of house-sitting—my first week of real adulthood—with failure.

When I saw the skunks, I was halfway down the driveway. The garbage can had been making a racket, echoing and rattling as it dragged behind me over the concrete. I didn't understand why the skunks hadn't startled. I didn't understand why I hadn't noticed them sooner.

There were three skunks, and they were babies. Each one followed right behind the other, noses glued to the dewy grass. Something in their walk reminded me of handheld vacuums, though this was a comparison I reached weeks later, lying in bed watching skunk YouTube videos.

A baby skunk, it turns out, is a grown-up in miniature. Scale is the only variable.

I'd never seen a baby skunk. The unseeing was different from the way I'd never seen a moose, or the northern lights. I hadn't been aware of waiting for them.

People who want to know more about the world have studied color. They've studied the way we see, think, and speak about it. If a language has two words for colors, those words will mean white and black. The other colors—the dandelions and the luna moths—still exist. So do the pieces of granite in the shade of a large pine tree in June. All of these things are called either "black" or "white."

There were three skunks. If a language has three words for color, the words will mean black, white, and red. Languages with five color words add green and yellow. Blue comes next, and is subsequently subdivided. In communities where light blue and dark blue have their own words, people are faster at telling the different shades apart. It's easier to see the things we have words for, though the blues go on existing.

The skunks did not have names. Sometimes they were together and sometimes they were apart. But they were never individuals, even when alone. In the same way that some languages happen to subdivide color into white, black, and red, this universe happened to subdivide the skunks into three bodies. In other universes it may be different. The skunks may have more or fewer bodies. Names confuse this. Names could make the skunks forget they are only segments of something larger.

Each skunk has a title: Eldest, Middle, and Third. They talk without speaking. The Middle Skunk flares the follicles at the base of her neck. The Third Skunk draws shapes in the air with his nose. We translate. *Please pass the grasshopper legs? I missed you, darling.*

Jan and Steve had two freezers: one in the kitchen, attached to the fridge, and one in the basement. In the long email of instructions—what day to put the trash out, where to find extra cat food, how to record the solar output at the end of the month—"the freezer" meant the freezer in the basement.

I was welcome to most of the food in the house, Jan wrote. It was just plain silly to have two bottles of ketchup in a single fridge! Though the email was signed "Jan and Steve," I felt sure it was Jan who had written it. The exclamation marks were one clue. Anything in the pantry—pretzels, pasta—was also fair game. They could always buy more. However, Jan asked that I leave the freezer untouched.

The emailer seemed embarrassed to set the limitation, which was another part of how I knew it was Jan. She tried to justify: the freezer was where they stored the food they made and grew themselves. They couldn't simply buy more homegrown blueberries upon returning home.

So the freezer took on an aura of mystique.

My father used to sing this song:

*Why did the kids put beans in their ears, beans in
    their ears, beans in their ears?*
Why did the kids put beans in their ears?
Because we told them no.

The first time I did laundry, I tiptoed to the freezer
after hitting start on the dryer. Something about the
deep grumble of hot air in a metal box made me feel
unseen. The zipper of a pair of jeans clinked against the
machine with each turn.

The freezer came up to my belly button. It was white
plastic, textured with shallow veins. I lifted the lid and
rested my forehead against the edge to hold it open. The
frozen blueberries were stacked in plastic bags along
the left edge. There were rainbow peppers, too, already
diced into stir-fry-able matchsticks. On the right side
stood towers of yogurt containers. The top one said
BEEF STOCK and the one next to it CHICKPEA KALE
SOUP. There were glass jars of pesto and tomato sauce.
In the middle of it all was a large shoebox.

I opened the shoebox, though I already knew it was
empty. The shoebox was part of the email.

Jan and Steve were hiking the Appalachian Trail. They
wouldn't do all of it, just what they could manage before
Steve had to return to teach high school environmental
science in the fall. The house would be mine for June,
July, and August. Jan and Steve wouldn't have access to

their phones. If something happened at the house, they wouldn't be reachable.

Jan and Steve had a cat. Her name was Athena. She was sleek and round, with fur like expensive upholstery. I'd met her once before that summer. If Athena died, I was supposed to put her body in the freezer. That was what the shoebox was for.

After I opened the freezer, I went to Jan's sewing room. Though the email gave it that name—she called it "my sewing room"—the room bore no traces of sewing. There were piles of paper, a stationary bike, and an empty glass terrarium about the right size for a newborn Komodo dragon. It was the sort of storage that happens gradually, building up in layers that might mean something to a geologist. The only thing that meant something to me was the curtains. They had trucks on them.

This is a story about a skunk who sometimes felt she should seek her fortune. She was the eldest of her siblings, and that came with some responsibility. She felt other things, too. She felt the grass between the pads of her paws—the grass that existed in layers. The green butter knives of the tips; the milky cylinders reaching up; the crinkled taupe of past years, waiting to decompose or be knitted into a starling's nest.

She felt hunger, and the urge to sneeze. She felt curiosity. Why did it give her pleasure to crunch a beetle between her teeth, and no pleasure at all to crunch a walnut shell? She felt love for her siblings, though that wasn't a feeling she ever noticed. That feeling was more like the feeling of having skin—so base level as to be unknowable. If your skin disappears, there is nothing left to feel with.

A beetle sat in the bottom layer of the grass. An oriole sat in the apple tree. Our story starts with the oriole, but he isn't any more important than the beetle.

Orioles migrate. They believe in forward motion, and the things that happened before happening again. Orioles can't fly backward, but they can fly in circles. The brightly colored ones arrived first each spring. They sang loudly from the treetops, having found their true loves. Their mates—the yellower, more muted birds—would be there soon, but their true loves were the apple trees. These were the days of passion. The shivering syrinx, the feathers growing thick and glossy in the joy. This lovely squatting bearer of buds. Its bark was nickel and naked, without many gnarls. Our oriole returned to the same one each year. Was the apple tree aware? No. Was the oriole embarrassed to love something that could not know it in return? No.

He saw the skunks, walking below his tree. He had seen the skunks before, though perhaps not these particular ones. Filled with his passion, and the urge to vomit up everything he knew so that the world might feed on it, he called out.

"Skunks," he sang, "let me tell you the difference between love and infatuation."

The skunks gathered around. They rubbed their noses against the trunk. They learned. Infatuation meant walking out into the middle of the open lawn. It meant they were not quite in the middle of the lawn, but far from where they had started and where they were going, with a certain knowledge of hawks aloft in unknown air currents. Love meant the end. It meant reaching the underside of a bush or porch. It meant deciding whether to take a bath or a nap.

The skunks understood that these were the seeds of definitions, and that their knowledge would need time to grow.

"Thank you, Oriole," they said.

They lifted their tails in unison and swished them once from left to right. It was like a ballet, or a windshield wiper.

Ellie and I went for a walk. We thought the line between childhood and adulthood was when you started to appreciate the pleasure of walking. In elementary school we'd done other things—tree climbing and stone soup making and deciding which last names, of all the last names on the planet, sounded best with our first names. Isabel Asgard or Isabel Reiner? Ellie Cook or Ellie Waterson-Williams?

Now I was a college graduate and she was a college dropout. We went for a walk.

It had just rained. Every time we got to a puddle I put my feet down slowly, heel to toe, so as not to splash. Ellie walked around the puddles.

Ellie was a person who would age gracefully. She'd stayed when the rest of us had left. For her the staying was an act in and of itself, rather than a lack of motion. Sometimes I looked at her—when we had agreed to meet at a café, and she got there first, and was sitting at the table not having seen me—and imagined how beautiful she would be with gray hair.

As we walked, Ellie talked about Sunday mornings. On Sunday mornings she took piano lessons from her old kindergarten teacher at the assisted living facility.

It's sort of like church, said Ellie, because religion is God acting through you. At least, my mom is a Quaker and that's how it is for Quakers. You sit and you wait until you think you know what God wants you to say and then you say it. And I think it's the same, with loving your neighbors and helping the poor, and singing hymns all together. You're doing the things He wants to do, but can't because He doesn't have a body. It's like that with Judy. Her fingers have a body, but it's a different body than what they used to have. She can't play the piano anymore. So Judy tells me what to do, and I make a lot of mistakes, but I'm trying. For God, and for Judy, the important thing is that you're trying. And it happens on Sunday mornings.

It's important to them that it happens on Sunday mornings?

No, no, she said. That's just another reason it's like church.

So that was Ellie for you. She had a little rain gauge inside her that was always full. Maybe behind the breastbone. In the rest of us, the rain gauge had a leak. We were always craving thunderstorms.

But how are you? said Ellie. She stretched her arms above her head for a second. Tell me something.

I told her I broke up with Henry. Ellie had never met Henry, but she heard about him whenever I was home on breaks.

Nothing was wrong, I said, but everyone else was making all these plans. They were moving to cities because of each other. They were making their partners' names into items that could be placed on a pro/con chart. I liked Henry a lot, but he felt like a person, not a factor.

Ellie nodded. And you feel okay about it?

I feel okay about it.

And that was, what, last month?

That was last month.

Next, Ellie wanted to know what happened yesterday.

Not much, I said. I saw some baby skunks.

Ellie stopped to pick a dandelion from someone's lawn.

Tell me more, she said.

She used her fingernail to slit a hole in the dandelion's stem and then bent down to pick another flower.

I tried to explain there was nothing to tell. I'd seen some skunks. I'd been restless all day. I kept opening the fridge and taking nothing out. It could have been a religious experience, except I didn't think the skunks had wanted me to act for them, or if they had, I hadn't gotten the message.

Ellie stood up again and crossed the street. The lawn over there hadn't been mowed as recently, so there were more dandelions. She asked if she could make an observation that might seem insulting, but she didn't mean it that way. Then she said she would just say it, because she hated when people asked for permission to say things. They were just trying to make themselves feel polite when actually they were being very rude.

I like these skunks, for you, she said. I think they signal a healthy new direction. Usually when you're home from college, all you talk about is boys. Like probably I can name more boys you've liked than classes you've taken. There's the one who always said hi in the dining hall, and the one who puts his hair up with a pencil. And that's fine. But you're not in college anymore, you know? You're single, and you're graduated, and you just saw some goddamn baby skunks.

Their hair, I said. Jesse puts their hair up with a pencil. Jesse uses they/them.

I tried to wipe some mud off the edge of my shoe and onto the grass. Ellie had six or seven dandelions strung together at this point. It was enough dandelions that they leapt around a bit every time the wind blew.

Right, she said. Jesse puts their hair up with a pencil. It's all the same: pronouns, these skunks. You have to practice good habits.

Two inches and two seconds away, a clover flexed its leaves, as if it had been sitting too long at its desk.

The Eldest Skunk froze. She made all her muscles wake up. A clock coalesced under her sternum, and she drew a line in the air with her nose. Slice of grass—clover—and two seconds farther, counted out by her insides. There, to the left of that dandelion. She pounced.

A beetle.

A beetle was love, not infatuation, she decided. Hours later, there would be bits of leg left to tongue from between her teeth.

So this was June—June as the first segment of something long and amorphous, instead of the opening of a carefully manicured three-act summer. House-sitting would end, and the rest of it—life—would keep on going. September no longer meant a return or a beginning. Or it might mean a beginning, but it was up to me to decide what would be beginning.

I applied for a few jobs. I didn't need a job—I wasn't paying rent, and I babysat occasionally—but I had to pass the time. The bookstore never replied and the donut shop wanted me to start at 3:00 AM. At the yoga studio, I sat on a folding stepladder while the current reception-ist explained the payment software. She was very preg-nant, and performed each action with one hand on one side of her belly and the other hand on the other side, as if the baby were a large bowl of soup that she needed to keep from dipping her sleeves in.

Students ebbed and flowed past the desk. They wore earth tones, or neon. One woman carried a mat with a repeating pattern of a talking snowman from a recent children's film.

The receptionist nodded to a person with short gray hair and a stainless steel water bottle. Hello, Linda! the receptionist said. Good class?

Linda paused in front of the desk. She sighed. Oh, she said, my sciatica is killing me. Last night I dreamed they took X-rays. In the dream they found a hard-boiled egg stuck in each hip flexor. I need to ask Roger about that. It might *mean* something.

The receptionist hummed in sympathy, if not agreement.

Linda hiked her yoga mat higher under her arm. Once she was gone, the receptionist turned to me, placing both hands on the right side of her belly.

That's Linda, she said. You have to watch out for her.

The thing about Linda was that she always tried to insert her credit card too soon. It messed up the whole transaction. Then you had to void it, and Linda would get suspicious that she was being charged twice. Luckily, there was an easy way to avoid this. The receptionist had learned to keep the credit card machine right beside her until she was ready. Then she could slide it across the desk to the student. This was the most reliable method—the method she recommended. She patted the machine protectively.

I wanted to tell her she would be a good mother, but maybe she already knew.

I'll email you the tax forms and everything, she said. And if questions come up, you can always call me. I won't be *gone*. I'm not *dying*.

Outside the building, it was sunny. I would be back in two Tuesdays, to sit in the swivel chair instead of on the stepladder. It was nice to have things to look forward to. On the bike ride home, the wind snuck in my sleeves at the wrists, traveling up my arms until it puffed out my shirt shoulders. The receptionist hadn't asked about my strengths or weaknesses, I realized. There'd been no moment to speak about a time I'd faced adversity, or to explain a tenuous connection between the yoga studio and my degree in anthropology. Oh well—so college didn't matter. I would be a person in a chair.

I wished they had said, "You're hired!" Sometimes it was nice to say things explicitly, instead of having them mutually understood. Sometimes people thought skipping over important questions would keep you from saying no.

I went to my father's house for dinner. He and Brigitte wanted to hear how I was doing. It had hardly been two weeks. Two weeks was no time at all compared to the semesters I'd spent at college, but it felt awkward now that we lived so close—like one of us was being avoided or forgotten. The daily rhythms of their life no longer included me, and hadn't for some time.

Brigitte was the reason I'd gotten the house-sitting job. She and Jan used to work together at a local green energy company. Jan did home visits and decided how many trees would need to be cut down to make room for the solar panels. Brigitte did marketing and designed the company lawn signs that went at the ends of people's driveways. They wore the same brand of hiking boots to the office each day. They stayed in touch even after Brigitte switched companies.

I put extra kibble in Athena's bowl before I left.

In my father's kitchen, Brigitte got me a glass of water. I hovered near the table. It was a different kitchen, a different house, from the one I'd grown up in. The table was the same, but it had been a debate if they would keep

Brigitte's table or my father's. My father chopped up a cucumber, transferred the slices to a plate, and wiped down the section of counter he'd been working at with a sponge. When I'd been small, he'd taught me to wipe counters with a rag. The sponge was Brigitte's influence. I tried to see it as a positive. He was in love; people were capable of change.

The cucumbers went in a salad with beets and feta. As we sat down to eat, Brigitte clapped a hand to her forehead.

I totally forgot! she said. You don't like feta, do you? I'm so sorry, I feel like an idiot.

No, no, I said. Feta is fine.

I was telling the truth. My taste buds had matured. Certain foods that used to trigger a gag reflex—feta, Swiss chard—were now pleasurable.

Really? said my dad. Who are you, and what have you done with my daughter?

The response confused me. He was acting as if he'd remembered my hatred of the cheese—as if it was a central aspect of my personality. But if he'd remembered, why had he served it to me? We were in his kitchen. The menu was under his control.

I didn't have much to report. The yoga studio job hadn't begun. Jan and Steve's roof hadn't sprung any leaks. I would be babysitting Cecelia later this week.

Brigitte nodded. And are you thinking about the fall?

I grimaced.

Sorry, sorry, said Brigitte. Don't listen to me—it's early.

We ate corn on the cob, and said all the things you had to say when eating corn: how good it tasted, how wonderful it was to live in a place where you could buy it at the side of the road.

My dad wiped his chin with a cloth napkin. He said a groundhog had been at his zucchini plants. He needed to figure out where the den was.

My father was in a constant war with the groundhogs. Every year, they ate his vegetables before the plants reached vegetable stage. Every year, he filled in their dens with dirt. Then the groundhogs dug though the dirt and ate more vegetables. Then my dad drove to the store, bought smoke bombs, stuck them down the dens, and blocked up the entrances.

Oh, I said. I *did* see some skunks at Jan and Steve's. That's something that happened.

My father whistled.

Skunks, he said. Skunks are hard. They don't always dig a hole—often they're just under a shed or something. Hard to fill that in. You could try a Havahart, but then how do you move it without them getting scared and spraying? It's a tough one. I'll have to think.

Brigitte brought out a rhubarb crisp before I could say anything else. I don't know what I would have said. How could I convince him that the skunks weren't a problem, that they didn't need a solution?

Have you seen Eli? asked Brigitte, looking through a drawer for dessert forks.

Eli was Jan and Steve's son. He was two years older than me, and we'd gone to the same high school. In the email, Jan wrote that Eli had some boxes stored in the closet of the sewing room. He was in the habit, she wrote, of stopping by to rifle through these boxes. Jan had given him my phone number. He was under strict orders to text me before doing any rifling. She hadn't given me Eli's number, and he hadn't texted.

I shook my head.

Brigitte looked surprised. She said she'd thought he was around—she'd thought he was working at that bakery in town.

I nodded. Eli did work at the bakery. But I hadn't seen him—we'd never been friends.

Brigitte got up to look for a serving spoon. She had a pie server on the table, but for some reason it wouldn't do.

I knew about the bakery from the social media accounts of Eli's and my old classmates. It was a bakery known for its sourdough. Eli had been tagged in multiple close-up photos of crumb structure. One of his friends had left a comment with a lewd pun about Eli's fondness for holes.

Brigitte held out a bowl of crisp for my assessment. More? Less?

I said it was perfect. I took a bite. It tasted the same as always. My father had made it. The recipe hadn't changed, or my taste buds hadn't aged out of the flavor.

Brigitte served my father a larger piece than she'd given me, and herself a smaller one. It annoyed me both that the portion sizes obeyed gender stereotypes, and that it wasn't Brigitte's fault—that was actually how much crisp we each wanted.

I always thought Eli was fairly good-looking, said Brigitte. But maybe I'm old and out of touch. I don't know what counts as cute these days.

I shrugged as if I hadn't thought about it. I didn't expect her to believe the shrug, only to take it as a sign that I didn't want to talk about it. My father, though, laughed.

See? he said to Brigitte. My daughter's got her head screwed on right. She's got better things to think about than cute boys.

In the dream, Orin pushed me down onto my back in the aisle of a bookstore. The carpeting itched under my shoulder blades as he kissed down my neck. I wanted to look at the light fixtures. I always liked kissing with my eyes open. It was like getting up early in the morning and having the whole house to yourself. But when I looked up to see what sort of lighting this bookstore used—chandeliers? track lights?—three of Orin's friends came down the aisle holding a video camera. They were above us, arcing the camera down to create the right perspective. It was some sort of documentary. They wanted to know if I would do an interview. Obviously the physical chemistry was there, but what about the emotional connection?

For a minute I was excited to get my makeup done for the interview, but then I looked around and Orin was gone.

I wanted to see Ellie but I didn't want her to think I was mooching her social scene. What was her social scene? She often ate pizza with her roommates, but beyond that I didn't have specifics. Then my phone buzzed. She asked if I wanted to volunteer at the library plant sale together. I said yes.

The idea was that people donated plants, and then other people, or the same people, paid money for the plants, and then the money went to the library. We sat in folding chairs by the side of the road and tried to be glad instead of nervous when cars slowed down. I'd brought a water bottle. Soon it was almost empty. I decided not to drink any more water until there were only twenty minutes left.

It was another Sunday afternoon. Ellie talked about how she had lost count of how many deer she'd seen on her trip to Vermont the week before. It had either been eleven deer or twelve deer. That was something she loved about Vermont—how you could lose count.

I picked a long blade of grass and tied it in knots.

Did you see any baby deer? I asked.

Ellie frowned. You mean fawns?

I shrugged. I never knew what I meant.

It was the season for fawns. But she hadn't seen any. Weird.

I held my water bottle up to my forehead like a plastic air-temperature ice pack. And how had her piano lesson gone, this morning?

Ellie kept her frown on. It was okay.

What was she learning, what piece was she working on?

She hummed a phrase. I recognized the tune, maybe from a movie soundtrack. It could have hid behind a shot of lush rolling hills.

It's Debussy, said Ellie, but it isn't going well. Judy's not a very good teacher. She's easily frustrated. Or not frustrated, exactly. More sad. And if she's sad, then I'm sad. She wants it to sound a certain way. Her fingers can't do it because she has arthritis, and my fingers can't do it because they're still learning, and we're both just using this crummy little electric keyboard that probably wouldn't sound right even if Yo-Yo Ma played it. So then we're both sad.

A red car drove by without slowing down.

Yo-Yo Ma is cello, I think, I said.

Ellie stopped frowning. Obviously. But probably he plays piano, too. Probably he plays like twelve instruments.

She hummed the phrase again, this time in a different key. It was unlikely she realized it was a different key. She wasn't very good at music. I tried not to be jealous of the arrangement. It was aspirational—to do the same thing with the same person every week, even though you were both bad at it. The badness proved you were doing it for each other instead of for the thing.

A blue Prius slowed down. Ellie and I were never nervous about blue Priuses. We always liked to laugh about how the plural of Prius might be Prii.

A man got out. He wasn't here to buy anything. He had donated a bunch of ornamental grasses to the sale and wanted to see how they were doing. If they were a hot-ticket item, so to speak, if they were selling like hot-cakes, then he had more at home that he could dig up and bring over. These grasses, he said, bred like rabbits.

The grasses were not selling. In fact we had not sold a single clump of grass. We had sold two aloe plants and a six-pack of basil seedlings. That was it.

Oh, he said. Well.

He browsed the vegetable table. Ellie and I tried not to look at each other. Then we had to look away so we wouldn't laugh. We'd heard about this man. The library director had warned us about him. Every plant sale, he donated more clumps of ornamental grasses than anyone knew what to do with. But he donated the grasses so earnestly. The library director never had the heart to tell him they were all ending up on her compost pile. Her compost pile, she said, which was overrun with ornamental grasses, because the man was right about one thing—they bred like rabbits.

This pepper, said the man suddenly, lifting up a pot. Do you know what type it is?

Ellie went over and took the pot from him. On a piece of masking tape on the side, it said PEPPER. She shrugged.

I'll take it, said the man. He was excited to solve the mystery. What would the pepper be when it grew up?

In the coming weeks, when I tried to rationalize my sudden feeling that a childhood home could also be an adult home, I thought about this man and his ornamental grasses. I imagined being known for something it had taken years to grow.

"Do you get bored?" asked the oriole.

If skunk communication is on one end of a spectrum, and words are at the other, orioles sing somewhere in the middle. They make noises through their mouths. The oriole didn't mean "bored," exactly. He was talking about the magnets in the tips of his wings. His children would hatch, and he would fly south.

The Eldest Skunk crouched next to the compost bin. Today it smelled of green banana peels and burnt toast, on top of the way it had smelled yesterday—moldy salsa—on top of the day before that.

"What are your magnets?" asked the oriole. He wasn't implying anything. He really wanted to know. He wanted to understand the world so he could care for it more accurately. "What do the bones of your inner ear whisper about when you sleep? Will they shuffle themselves around at some point, and declare a new *up*?"

The Eldest Skunk closed her eyes. In her ears was the wind, rattling the green pine needles in the tree above her. She rolled over in the grass and curved her spine like a crescent moon.

The oriole told her a story about three pigs. The first pig built a house of straw, the second a house of sticks, and the third a house of stone. Maybe you've heard the story before. The Eldest Skunk hadn't.

"We sleep under the forsythia," she explained. That was her house.

She nosed at the black plastic of the compost bin. The plastic gave her a bad feeling, but she also felt that there was something good inside. The compost was the only place she ever felt shame, and she kept coming back.

A thought scuttled by. "Don't pigs like mud?" the skunk asked the oriole.

He agreed that they did.

"Why didn't the pigs build their houses out of mud?"

The oriole flew a few inches into the air, and then perched again on a lower twig. That was his point exactly. "Their inner ear bones must have rearranged themselves," he said. "It must have been the magnets."

The oriole loved this feeling—a meeting of minds. He flew back to the apple tree before anything could spoil it.

At night the skunks slept in a big pile. They stopped being three skunks, and became twelve legs and three tails. Any given patch of fur could be categorized as self, pillow, or blanket.

They didn't need bedtime stories. Every day the leaves on the forsythia above them grew bigger, until they started falling off instead. The branches curved up and over, forming an arc.

The Eldest Skunk could feel the three pigs stuck in her throat. How could she get them out in the open? Her mouth couldn't make the same noises as the oriole's. Eventually, she asked her siblings what a fortune looked like.

A fortune?

A future, a calling, an expedition to build a different house.

But we have a house.

Exactly. That's what's been bothering me.

They tossed the thoughts around like balloons that were not allowed to hit the ground. The moon was halfway between new and full that night. The Eldest Skunk couldn't remember which direction it had been moving in.

Waxing, her siblings knew. She relaxed. Sleep fell over them like a maple leaf in autumn—graceful and blazing red.

When it was the Middle Skunk's turn to dream, she dreamed of branches snapping suddenly behind her. Over and over, she lifted her tail only to find herself reasonless. There was no source to the noise, and nothing to aim at. By the driveway there was a mailbox. In the forest there was a fallen log. Without motion, an item had no teeth.

Her tail was getting tired of all this up and down—in the dream. Surely there were alternative responses to stimuli. What did other creatures do when their pulse sped up? Did they fly away? Did they fall in love?

The pile of legs and tails rebraided itself. The Third Skunk took over the dream. He dreamed of moths. The moths stayed alive from generation to generation by matching their wings to the bark on the trees. The hawks kept looking past them because of the matching colors. The moths kept having babies because they weren't getting eaten. But then the moths were gone, and there were snowflakes instead. The trees were gray. The snowflakes were white. The snowflakes felt brilliant and afraid of their individuality, like a flock of teenage girls at the mall. They needed a skunk. A wide white stripe could be a home.

Days passed. The skunks ate green blueberries that the mockingbirds had spat to the ground. A human mowed the lawn when the sun was high and the skunks were asleep. In the twilight, the skunks raised their feet high off the ground. Their ankles were damp with the blood of the grass. The air inside their ears and noses was pungent with green: moss, jade, pear. Shamrock, seaweed, olive, seafoam, underripe tomato, overgrown spinach. They broke from the single-file line to frolic this way and that.

I set an alarm for half an hour before sunrise.
A sunrise was about the lead-up, not the peeking over the horizon. The time the weather app called "sunrise" came long after the most interesting colors. Though the colors weren't my goal, I needed to be awake before the light.

In the kitchen I measured instant coffee into a travel mug without turning on the lights. I'd slept fitfully. Whenever I'd reached for my phone to see if it was late enough to count as getting up early instead of getting up in the middle of the night, the numbers had been almost the same as before. Then I would regret the reach—it had woken my arm; it had exposed me to blue light. I pushed the lid onto the travel mug. My eyelashes were stuck together in one corner.

The skunks needed a physical dimension. A crush couldn't survive as pure idea. Jan and Steve had a half-empty bag of sunflower seeds in the pantry, but I resisted. I had to manage expectations.

Outside, I shuffled once around the lawn in bare feet. The grass had been cut the day before and the wet clippings stuck to my ankles. Every so often I squatted down to look under a bush. Back at the front steps, I sat down to wait for my ankles to dry.

In the movies I'd watched as a child, there were two mainstays: woodland animals eating from the hands of beautiful girls, and handsome princes falling in love with beautiful girls. I wasn't an idiot, as a child. I knew that woodland animals didn't eat from people's hands. It stood to reason that a boy falling in love with me was just as far-fetched. Being a beautiful girl would have to be enough of a reward in and of itself.

The cold seeped through the seat of my jeans, and the sun, pooling on my cheekbones, curdled as it reached my eyes. My phone buzzed against my butt. I switched it to silent mode without taking it out of my back pocket, fingers worming between the phone and the denim.

Still, it was nice to think about. What would it feel like, for a skunk to press its nose into the space between my index finger and thumb? In my head, a skunk traced its nose down my knuckles, pausing at each divot. In my head, its nose felt like the tip of an underripe strawberry. Supermarket strawberries were never quite ripe. They were red except for the ends, which were still pale. The ends were cool and soft and harder than you expected.

Even if people had been explaining it to me my whole life—what it felt like to have a skunk trace its nose across your palm—I imagined I wouldn't be ready. To be ready would ruin everything. If it was pleasant or unpleasant was beside the point: a skunk had eaten sunflower seeds from your hand.

Across the street, in the neighbors' driveway, a robin hopped up and down. A man pedaled by on a recumbent bicycle, with NPR playing quietly from a Bluetooth speaker. At the foot of the porch steps stood a single dandelion, gone to seed. I picked it and pursed my lips. When I blew, the seeds went nowhere. They were too green, too stuck.

The grass on my ankles dried and the skunks did not appear. I pulled out my phone. The text was from a new number. It had been sent at 6:37 AM. The author needed his tennis racket and wondered if he might stop by to pick it up sometime today. He didn't want to play tennis, but the deal was that if he played tennis with Rachid, Rachid would play Frisbee with him. Signed, Eli.

I didn't know who Rachid was.

sure, I typed, *anytime.* My phone autocorrected *sure* to *Sure*, but I changed it back. Eli's message hadn't had any capital letters.

lit, said Eli two minutes later. *i'll b there at 1 ish.*

The "lit" wasn't a good sign, but I had already forgiven the skunks for not being where I wanted them to be.

●

At 1:16 Eli rang the doorbell. He was wearing a blue bike helmet. I'd wanted to be washing lunch dishes when he arrived, but there had only been a plate and a knife and a cutting board. Now they were in the drain rack.

Hi, I said, opening the door.

Hey, he said, sorry about this. I really need to stop using this place as like, a storage unit. It's probably not very adult of me.

I mean, I said, it's fine. It's your parents' house.

That it was me doing the house-sitting, and not Eli, made very little sense. He was paying money to live in an apartment on one side of town, and his parents were paying me to live here. Maybe it had to do with independence and self-differentiation. Maybe he'd already signed his lease by the time Jan and Steve decided to travel.

I opened the door wider so he could come in. He took off his bike helmet as if he were entering a church. His hair was curlier than it had been in high school. Or maybe it was just shorter. We'd been in chorus together, but I'd known who he was before that. Everyone knew who Eli was. It was a sort of personality quiz—if you thought he or Ryan was hotter. I always said Ryan. The question got asked a lot, whenever a group of girls wanted to feel more intimate with each other.

Eli's house—suddenly it stopped being Jan and Steve's house, in my head, and became Eli's—started with a mudroom. The mudroom funneled into a narrow hallway, and the narrow hallway burst out into the kitchen. I didn't know which of us would walk down the hallway first. Eli moved before I did. He kept walking through the kitchen and up the stairs, two at a time, without saying anything or looking back. I studied the magnets on the fridge. One of them was shaped like a yellow rubber duck, about an inch tall. It occurred to me that Eli might have been the one to choose this magnet. I picked up a dish towel and started drying the plate from lunch.

Eli came back into the kitchen carrying Athena. Maybe it's in the garage, he said.

It wasn't clear if he was talking to me or to himself or to Athena. He leaned against the counter instead of going toward the garage, but he was looking at that cat, not at me. I finished drying the plate and put it in the cupboard.

Do you want a glass of water? I asked. The question was a gift to myself—I knew he wouldn't understand the reference.

He looked up. Oh, no, thanks. I should be going.

Athena leapt out of his arms. He went into the garage. I dried the knife and the cutting board. It occurred to me that the rest of the day would pass very slowly.

Fuck, said Eli, coming back into the kitchen for the second time. Did they get rid of my tennis racket?

I shrugged. Do you want help looking?

No, no. He shook his head. I don't even like tennis. I'll just tell Rachid it's a sign from the universe.

Athena rubbed up against his ankles. She was never this affectionate with me. He squatted down to pet her. Do *you* like tennis? he asked suddenly, looking up.

I shook my head. I'd never even held a tennis racket.

Rats. That would have been better. Then you could've played Rachid, and I wouldn't have to.

Sorry, I said. I considered suggesting that Rachid could give me lessons. It wasn't that I didn't like tennis, only that I'd never tried it. A year before, I would have stayed silent because I was too shy. Today I stayed silent so as not to give myself more boys to think about.

Eli stood up, dusting his hands on his thighs. Well, he said, sorry for the intrusion.

He hadn't intruded. He'd only made me feel like an intruder. I said it was nothing, it was his house, he could stop by anytime.

He insisted it wasn't his house, it was his parents' house. He had his own place.

It was both understandable to want to make this distinction and utterly pointless.

Actually, he said, my house is having a little cookout thing on Friday, if you want to come.

I gripped my elbows with my opposite hands. I have to babysit, I said. I tried to convey disappointment without conveying the full extent to which I was disappointed. I really had to babysit. Jon and Amelie were going to see the new Batman movie. Batman was the only superhero Amelie liked. He was so noir. I would put Cecelia to bed and eat one of the mini Häagen-Dazs ice cream bars from their freezer.

Eli scratched his ear. Well, he said, I hope you're having a good summer. Honestly, I kind of hated it when I moved back. Like, it felt weird to need to start over, socially, in a place I've always been.

I nodded slowly. It felt strange. My strangeness and Eli's strangeness were probably different feelings, but it was nice to imagine they were the same.

The summer after my freshman year of college, I'd seen a boy from my ninth-grade PE class in an airport across the country. I hadn't been able to remember his name. We'd run toward each other and hugged. Having gone to high school together, it turned out, meant something. There was a sense that these people had known who you were before *you* knew who you were, and that you could be honest with each other.

I guess I just got back, I said. Like, I haven't been here long enough for being alone to mean being lonely. I don't know. I go on hikes.

I tucked my hands behind me, between the edge of the counter and my tailbone. I'd been picking at the skin at the side of my fingernail.

Eli looked at home in a way that had nothing to do with whose house we were in. His arms hung like cotton shirts fresh from the dryer—loose without limpness. He looked like he really believed what I was saying.

Hikes, he said. Hikes are major. I remember that.

I laughed, and he laughed too.

Just let me know, he said, if you want to get coffee or something.

Then he left. A minute later he was back, without knocking, half jogging through the kitchen and up the stairs. I forgot my bike helmet!

Then he was gone for real. I turned around once in place. I wanted to turn on the tap and stick my head under the faucet. Instead I put my phone face down on a windowsill and vacuumed the whole house without listening to music.

There are metaphors for skunks: the bubbles in the electric teakettle before the automatic shutoff kicks in. A mountain lake with a snowbank sticking out of it. Water so clear you can't tell how deep it goes. Drugs. Medicine. Hot spaghetti with refrigerator-temperature red sauce after a long day of physical labor. An old woman in pink tweed with a stuffed bird on her hat. Chrysanthemums.

Dear Ellie,

I went to the library today. It was a new library for me, since Jan and Steve live one town over from the house I grew up in. Some things are always the same, though: the circulation desk, the computer for catalog searching that's so old the "F" and "J" have worn off their keys from all the fingers. I typed in "skunks." I think I wanted to need to use the Dewey decimal system. I wanted to be given a number that said This is where you are. This is a place people have been before, and here are some topics next door to you. *Instead, all the call numbers sent me to the young readers room. There was a book about a skunk having a birthday party, and one about a skunk becoming friends with a badger. As a topic, skunks seem to be more next door to unicorns than biology. I filtered for "nonfiction" and it turned out one result: a National Geographic Kids book on woodland animals. It was unavailable. I'm trying to cultivate that skunk-feeling, but it's not working. A mother herded her small child away from me, even though I smiled at them, and the water fountain was broken. I checked out a book called* The Skunk *because it was hardest to tell, from the cover—a cartoon man looking over his shoulder; a city skyline—what the plot would be. I haven't read it. Probably you will tell me to be patient. I can accept that as long as you don't say a garden doesn't grow overnight.*

I traced the cap of the pen around my chin. There was nothing else to say. I closed my notebook. My journal entries were all addressed to my female friends. It was the only way to trick myself into knowing what was worth writing down.

Cecelia and I walked to the woods near her house. I had a backpack with Cheerios, apple slices, *The Skunk*, and *Cinder Edna*. I needed to share the skunks with someone. Part of the fun of boys was that you could tell stories about them to other people and the other people would find it exciting, at least at first. Cecelia was four. Even if it was too late for me, maybe it wasn't too late for her.

She held my hand while we crossed the street. I tried to remember what it was like to have to reach up to hold a hand. Our shoulders were having completely different experiences.

We put wood chips on dry leaves and set them in the stream. Cecelia said her boat was going to China. I picked Seattle. There was an eddy. The boats kept coming back to where they started.

We must have made baby boats by accident, said Cecelia. They aren't ready to leave their parents. We have to take them back with us.

The leaves were crinkling apart and dripping, but they got zipped into the outside pocket of the backpack.

Cecelia insisted this was the only way they would feel safe.

There was a wide flat rock where we always sat for books and snack. *Cinder Edna* was a retelling of *Cinderella*. Edna and Ella are neighbors. Edna makes her own dress and takes the bus to the ball. She marries the prince's younger brother, and they start a recycling plant behind the castle.

I wanted to read *The Skunk* next. Cecelia wanted *Cinder Edna* again.

Why? I asked.

Because it's good.

But why is it good?

Daddy says its fem-nist. She flicked her hair behind her ear. This was a gesture she hadn't had the summer before.

Hmm, I said, swatting at a mosquito. But it still ends with her getting married.

No, it doesn't, said Cecelia. It ends with a recycling plant. You obviously weren't paying attention. We need to read it again.

I wiped some pine needles off the rock and lay down on my stomach. Cecelia sat on the small of my back. She wanted to "braid" my hair. There was a pebble digging into my hip bone and I didn't move. At camp, my favorite day was always the first, when they sat us down on stools and combed through our hair for lice, plastic teeth drawing pictures into our scalps. It sent tingles down my arms.

I read *The Skunk* out loud to myself and Cecelia pretended not to listen.

The Skunk was about a man who lives in a city. One day he notices he is being followed by a skunk. He turns left. He turns right. He locks his apartment door and takes a detour through the sewers. Still—the skunk. He asks what it wants, but maybe the skunk doesn't speak English or doesn't know what it wants, or maybe there is a skunk word for what it wants with no adequate English translation. The skunk stays silent.

I could feel my rib cage expanding on the rock every time I turned a page. Cecelia kept her fingers at the ends of my hair, away from the scalp. She didn't interrupt.

Eventually the man moves to a new apartment. He rents a big truck and has a housewarming party. Something is missing. A woman's ponytail takes on a skunk-like aspect. The black-and-white awning of a café makes his intestines leap. He squares his shoulders and stands on his new stoop.

When it was over, I asked Cecelia what she thought.

Did you bring a hair tie? she asked. She had my hair twisted up in a sort of cinnamon bun over my left ear.

No, sorry.

She let my hair go all at once. Let's read *Cinder Edna* again, she said.

I didn't argue. In the pictures, Cinderella's prince was very blond and square jawed. The jaw was always tipped a little upward. If you put a marble on his tongue, it would have rolled right down into his small intestine.

My dad loaned me that book that everyone was reading about the grasses. It was about other plants, too, but the grasses had the most symbolic weight. They were different from the grasses in our lawn, and different from the ones at the plant sale. Humans were forgetting how to take care of them. The book had made my father cry, but he didn't approve of people who watered their lawns. It was a waste of water.

For a little while life didn't seem to have
anything to do with Eli.

I arrived at 8:20 AM on my first day at the yoga studio. The previous receptionist had recommended 8:30. The key didn't stick in the lock, and the alarm system flashed a green light after I entered the code. Inside, I sat on the swivel chair. It left my heels a half inch above the floor. I reached down for the lever on the side and lowered the seat. Now I had to sit up extra straight to feel any sense of authority over the empty room.

The first class of the day was Pilates. Though I thought of it as a "yoga" studio in my head, they also offered meditation, Zumba, and Pilates. Was there a word that encompassed all these things? Should it be called a "movement" studio? But meditation didn't involve movement. The uniting factor was more abstract, and had something to do with self-improvement.

The Pilates teacher, Stacy, arrived at 8:45.

Hi, she said, waving one hand next to her shoulder in a frantic hello. I'm Stacy.

Stacy was tiny in a way that obviously came from her bones. Pilates wouldn't make you look like her, and there was no tricking yourself into thinking it would. She had bleached blonde hair, grown out enough for the dark roots to make a circle around her face, like a little annotation in a book: *Here is a face!* She was surprised I hadn't set up the fans. The studio didn't have air conditioning. Instead, she explained, they relied on a complex arrangement of electric fans. We unlocked the storage closet and stared at the fans. They stared back. It was a lot of fans. Stacy walked me through the studio, pointing to certain places on the floor that were marked with electrical tape. Those were the spots where the fans went.

And then, she said, another fan goes on the folding chair, and the folding chair goes in the doorway between the studio and lobby.

She clicked the Bluetooth button on the speaker, scrolling through her phone with the other hand. Her nails were long and pink. They were the sort of nails people spent hours in salons to have applied, or the kind that people used as an excuse for spending hours in salons, unable to turn the pages of a magazine.

But obviously we don't really set up the folding chair until class has started, she said, so people can still go through the doorway. Then she looked up at me, like *Any questions?* but also like she couldn't imagine what possible question I would have. She'd given me all the necessary information. She wanted to scroll her phone in peace.

I got started on the fans. Yoga blocks were also part of it—they got wedged underneath the window sashes to encourage airflow. At this point in the morning, it was still cool outside, but it was important to be prepared.

While I worked, Stacy retied her ponytail twice. Then she laid out a selection of what looked like giant rubber bands on the floor by the mirror.

So what's your deal? she asked. College student?

There were a couple of colleges in the area, and sometimes people moved here for them. I shook my head. I grew up here.

She nodded and picked up her phone again.

I hadn't accurately described my situation. Now the moment had passed. She probably thought I was younger than I was, or that I hadn't been to college at all.

When the students came in, Stacy greeted each one by name. How was Ethan liking soccer camp, she wanted to know? Had Carmen figured out which cat was leaving the dead birds in the garden clogs?

Most people had prepaid class cards. I didn't have to use the credit card machine, only initial next to their names on the sign-in sheet. They paused at the clipboard without looking at me, then floated onward into the studio. Did anyone notice I was new? Did anyone notice I wasn't pregnant?

The class, when it finally began, was like a radio program. If I swiveled my chair to the side, I could see Stacy through the open door, on the other side of the box fan. I stayed facing the desk. Everything was noise.

I didn't know much about Pilates. It was something people did to try and look hotter. That made it embarrassing—a confession of vanity. It meant you'd been infected by capitalist beauty standards. True hotness could only be achieved by hiding the work that went into it. Pilates might make you look hot to a person across the bar who didn't know how you'd spent your Tuesday 9:00 to 10:00 AM hour, but once they understood that your beauty came from a set of carefully curated exercises and didn't emanate mysteriously from your soul, the ruse would be up.

Stacy wanted everyone to take a moment to choose an affirmation. Maybe they wanted to feel strong. Maybe they wanted to let go of something. Maybe they wanted to honor the feedback their body was giving them, and take the modifications in today's class.

Take these wants, said Stacy, and phrase them as something that's already true. I *am* strong. I *will* honor my body's feedback. Let's go around, she said, and share our affirmations—if you feel comfortable. Meredith, you start.

Meredith wanted to feel in control. What she said was "I am in control," but I knew how to reverse translate because of Stacy's directions. Meredith wasn't in control.

Maggie wanted to take this hour to focus on just herself, rather than her family. Her husband clearly never unloaded the dishwasher.

I wasn't kind to these women, in my head. Their sincerity shocked me. Didn't they know to roll their eyes at this sort of thing?

Kaz wanted a rounder butt. I will have a peachy booty, she said.

I liked Kaz.

Stacy laughed generously with everyone else. You *will*, she said, but we try to make these affirmations internal.

We try to focus on how our bodies *feel* rather than how they *look*. Do you want to add a second affirmation, something internal?

A moment of silence passed. I watched the second hand on the wall clock above the door. It ticked from slightly beyond the two to slightly before the three. Why did we assume Kaz meant peachiness in an external, rather than internal, way?

I am brave, said Kaz.

The exercises all had industrial-sounding names. There were fire hydrants and oil riggers and planks and bridges. It was like being on a construction site. I played a game where I would close my eyes and try to guess what each exercise looked like, then open my eyes and turn my chair slightly to the left to check. Stacy raised and lowered her chest to the floor, elbows tucked in next to her body. I googled "oil rig" on my phone. Stacy looked like a grasshopper, not an oil rig. I googled "Pilates." Pilates was a man, it turned out. His first name was Joseph.

Stacy said we had to stop thinking of our spines as one unit. She wasn't including me in her "we," and wasn't talking about my spine. I closed my eyes to listen closer. She said we couldn't take any of our vertebrae for granted. We were going to paint our spines down onto the floor, one inch at a time, leaving no gaps. This was part of a motion known as a "bridge."

Pretend, said Stacy, that you're a skunk. Make sure every inch of your stripe is touching the floor! Imagine your tail, stretching beyond your tailbone!

I opened my eyes.

After class, Stacy said she hoped having the door open hadn't been a distraction for me.

No, I said, not at all. I liked it. I'd never heard a Pilates class before.

She blushed. It's so silly, isn't it?

No, really, I said.

Pilates *was* silly, but if Stacy found it embarrassing, that was just depressing. Had the sincerity of the women's affirmations been a ruse?

It was interesting, I insisted. Poetic, even. That thing about the skunk, and the spine.

Stacy groaned. God, she said, shaking her head. I hate the skunk thing.

Once, years ago, Stacy had been taking a class where the teacher used the skunk analogy. *That is so dumb*, Young Stacy had thought to herself. The image didn't even help. It would be more efficient to tell people to imagine they had a stripe down their back and leave the woodland animals out of it. But then Older Stacy had become a Pilates teacher, and found herself saying it.

I always tell myself I'm not going to say it, she said, and then it's time for bridges, and I'm running out of things to say, and out it comes. It's so bad. Like, I quit cigarettes. But I can't quit this.

I was glad she hadn't quit. I liked the skunks. Their presence felt like the universe nodding its head in approval.

I went hiking by myself. Hikes were different from walks. Walks happened near roads and houses, and were about appreciating your humanness: front doors could be orange, and humans were the ones who had made them that way. Hikes happened in the woods, and were about forgetting your humanness.

It was the first real hike I'd been on since moving back—I'd lied to Eli. I was trying to be honest in retrospect. He'd said hikes were major. I was taking his advice.

I walked through a spiderweb. It was unavoidable, stretching unseen across the path. The trail was one my father used to bring me to. I'd always made him go in front—that way he was the one who hit the spiderwebs. I wondered how many he'd walked through without comment, trying to convince me the woods were a benevolent place. Back then I'd hated hiking.

I ran my hands down my arms again and again. The feeling was still there. The spiderweb was still pressed against my skin, between my arm hairs.

The trail intersections looked familiar, but seemed to show up in a different order than they had in my childhood. Had the vernal pool always been so close to the birch grove?

The birches gave way to beech trees. Beech trees were my favorite. The sunlight that came through their leaves had a different texture. It was like the drop of sap that welled up when you cut the stem of a daffodil. When had I learned what made a beech tree a beech tree? There was the smooth gray bark, and the teeth around the edges of the leaves. I knew the knowledge came from my father, though I couldn't pinpoint how or when. He liked to compare the trunks to elephant legs. Neither of us had ever seen an elephant.

Two squirrels played tag in the trees above me. Every so often one of them slipped, fell, and landed on a lower branch. For a minute it seemed like I, too, was part of their game. The trees they leapt between followed the path.

My phone buzzed. Hikes were the time it was both easiest and stupidest to be without your phone. What if you got lost? What if you were injured?

Yooooo.

The text was from Ellie.

I'm going to Vermont again this weekend, do you want to go visit Judy for me?? Pretty please???

Another message: *She will be lonely :(*

And another: *You can learn piano!!!*

When I looked up, the squirrels had disappeared. Maybe they had noticed their third player had dropped out, or maybe I had never been part of it to start with.

On Sunday morning, I put on the River Valley Co-op tee with the little holes around the neckline and went to Judy's. I was proud of the holes. They proved my love for the shirt. At the assisted living facility, the receptionist wore teal cat-eye spectacles. They were so teal I had to look away and then back again. They didn't seem like something that belonged to real life.

I wrote *piano lesson* in the *reason for visit* spot. This was a mistake. The residents, the receptionist informed me, were not allowed to provide services for monetary gain out of their rooms. It was a zoning issue.

Oh, I said, but there's no monetary gain. I'm not paying Judy money. I can't even play piano.

She frowned. Then why are you here?

To visit.

Yes, but what is your *reason for visit*? She spoke slowly and pointed at the words at the top of the column in the guest book, as if this was a "learn to read" situation. Eventually we crossed out *piano lesson* and squeezed in *social* above it. Room 211, she said. She wasn't happy about it.

Welcome mats lay outside some of the residents' doors. A line of porcelain hedgehogs stood guard on the narrow sill above 204. Were the people with bare doors the same ones who had left their lockers undecorated over half a century before? Or did tastes evolve? At 211, I wondered if I had remembered the number wrong. A magazine cutout of Cindy Crawford in a gold swimsuit was taped over the peephole. Cindy's gaze had a strong handshake. She would be disappointed in me if I didn't knock soon. I knocked.

Judy opened the door right away. She wore leopard print leggings and a sparkly headband.

I was just doing my exercises, she said, pointing at the headband. Then she demonstrated how she was supposed to hold on to the kitchen counter and move her legs back and forth. She had a collection of Jane Fonda workouts on VHS, but her physical therapist said they weren't appropriate for her stage of life. So the VHS tapes were looking for a good home. Did I want them?

I don't have a VHS player, I said. Judy was already someone I wanted to model myself after, but not for her VHS tapes. And I really didn't have a VHS player.

Judy's apartment was tiny and tiled in linoleum. A love seat the color of dead leaves filled one wall of the living room. A magnet on the fridge, in the kitchenette, said IT'S WINE O'CLOCK. I looked for something to say.

Well, I said at last, it's nice to finally meet you. I've heard so much from Ellie.

Oh, good, said Judy. I love to be talked about. It happens so rarely once you're old—that's why it's better to be famous.

Her voice had a crackle I associated with my grand-mother, who'd died when I was ten. Suddenly I understood that the crackle might have been more a feature of age than personhood. Judy's words came quickly, as if they, too, were wearing leopard print leggings.

Following her directions, I extracted the piano from behind the love seat and unfolded it. She asked if I knew how to type. It felt like a trick question. How to *properly* type, said Judy, with your fingers on the home row.

I sat on a stool, and she stood behind my right shoulder. I knew about the home row, but couldn't think if it was something I used, the same way I couldn't remember where the important buttons in a car were unless I was sitting in a driver's seat. Letters appeared on the screen without me thinking about it.

This, said Judy, reaching around me to press a white key in the middle of the board, is middle C. This is your home row.

I put my index finger over the note she had pressed, pretending it was the *J* on my laptop. No, no, said Judy. She arranged my fingers herself, placing my thumb over middle C and curling the other fingers onto their respective keys. Her skin made me not believe in opposites. It was soft and rough at once.

We played a scale. Judy said the letters out loud as I pressed each note. It was like learning the alphabet all over again. I could see how she would have been a good kindergarten teacher—in her mouth, the letters all sounded like they wanted to be your friends.

I wasn't good. Judy kept poking at my wrists, positioning them in ways that didn't feel any different from how I'd had them before. There was a point in the scale where I was supposed to tuck my thumb under to reach the next note, which I couldn't do without breaking rhythm, even at half speed.

At the piano, Judy might have been naked. Anything extra—in her voice, her movements, the path of her eyes—vanished. I remembered what Ellie had said about Quaker meeting. It was easy to take guided meditation seriously if no one laughed.

How much time was passing? At a certain point I asked for a glass of water. We were still practicing scales. The rush of tap water sounded like Cecelia's white noise machine. I asked what Ellie had been like in kindergarten.

Judy handed me the glass of water before answering. She extended a finger and played a single note—one of the black keys at the right end of the keyboard. The same, I think, she said slowly. Most people are the same. There was a month when we had to check her pockets after recess, because she kept bringing woolly bears inside. I still don't know where she found them all. But she was the same. Now play the scale again.

The scale wasn't any better this time.

Eventually Judy said it was enough for today. Did I want to stay for tea?

I did. We boiled water and arranged a packet of wafer cookies in a star pattern on a plate. I put away the piano and sat down on the front quarter of one of the love seat cushions.

Judy asked what kind of tea I wanted and then said never mind, she only had Irish breakfast. She sat next to me on the love seat, farther back on the cushions. I balanced my mug on my knee. The cookie plate covered the whole top of the stool where I'd sat during the piano lesson. We laughed to break the silence. What were we waiting for? It reminded me of internet dates in college, when a boy and I would sit on a bed making small talk, trying to silently agree about when the kissing would start.

So, I said, have you always lived here?

Nova Scotia. Judy smiled. Her voice put its clothes back on. I didn't understand how she could be two separate people in the space of an hour and still say that people stayed the same between kindergarten and adulthood.

I grew up in Nova Scotia, she said, sitting up straighter. Then I came here for college. Then I met Jim.

I didn't have to ask for more. The Jim story was a story Judy knew how to tell.

At first, Judy and Jim were just friends. Acquaintances, really. Then one night, she and her friends were in a restaurant, and this group of guys had a table on the other side of the room. So Judy and her friends kept looking but not looking. Do people still do that, Judy wanted to know? She hoped they did. One of her friends liked the redhead, and another preferred the one with the beard. There was one boy sitting so they couldn't see his face. He was just a cowlick and a pair of shoulder blades. That one, Judy said to her friends. I like those shoulder blades. She said it mostly to make her friends laugh. When they all got up to leave, the shoulder blades belonged to Jim.

I laughed. It was a good story even if I wasn't the first to hear it.

Judy showed me pictures of Jim in her photo album, and I pulled up photos of Henry on my phone. Nice eyebrows, said Judy.

Eli had nice eyebrows, too. There weren't any photos of him in my camera roll, so I didn't bring him up. It was easier to tell Judy there weren't any people of interest right now, and that I hadn't met anyone since getting home. In a few ways, it was the truth. I'd met Eli long before this summer. Nothing was going on.

Judy's pages of shiny paper felt so much more permanent than the images on my screen, though people insisted everything that happened on the internet was there forever. In the photo album, we moved backward in time. Jim was gray-haired and then Jim was brown-haired. Then he was reading a book to a small child; then he was spitting out a mouthful of spaghetti. One photo was taken from behind, on a mountain. His shoulder blades were underneath his backpack.

You should come next week, too, said Judy, picking up another cookie. Ellie never wants to talk about men.

I nodded. The tea was oversteeped in a way that stuck to the back of my throat. On my way out the door, I gave Cindy a little wave.

What did it all mean? There were the skunks and the boys, the Ellies and Judies. Ellie had sent me here, but I didn't think she would have approved of the conversation Judy and I were having. Don't you think it's sad? she would have asked. That Judy has lived a whole long interesting life, and what she most wants to talk about is men?

I tried to feel the sadness of it. Mostly I thought: Imagine. Imagine a single person being more interesting than all the rest of your life combined! That would be a very interesting person. I wanted to meet a person like that.

I went back to Cecelia's.

Come on, she said, come on.

She didn't even let me take my shoes off. We had to go right back outside.

She's been asking for you all morning, said Jon. Jon was Cecelia's father. His work was something that happened from home and was related to podcasts. When he shrugged, it jostled the earphones resting around his neck.

Cecelia and I stood on her stoop. I asked where we were going and if we should bring snacks.

No snacks. We're going for a walk.

The sun leaned over us, watching. I let Cecelia pull me along the sidewalk. She lifted her feet slightly higher than normal with each step. At intersections she looked behind us before looking left, right, left. Eventually we got to the park with the slide where she liked to play "the wood chips are lava."

Did she want to play?

No.

Did she want me to push her on the swings?

Cecelia let go of my hand and spun in a circle, eyebrows lowered. How do we get to the sewers? she asked.

The what?

The sewers.

I squatted down next to her. It was as if two pages had stuck together, and the story had skipped ahead without my realizing it. We can't go to the sewers, I explained. The sewers aren't for people.

I didn't even know if our town had a sewer system. The house I had grown up in used its own tank.

Cecelia stomped her foot. Yes, they are! The man in the book—he went to the sewers.

What book?

She rolled her eyes in four steps: look left, look up, look right, look down. She had just learned about eye-rolling and needed practice.

You know, Isabel. The skunk book! I want to find the skunk!

I sat back on my heels. Whenever people asked me why I liked babysitting, I cited the element of surprise.

Well, I said. That was a book. Books aren't real. People don't normally go in sewers, and skunks definitely don't.

Then where is he?

It had been stupid to not bring snacks. She was going to cry. I think he's asleep, I said. Skunks are crepuscular—it means they're mostly awake at dawn and dusk.

That was something the internet had told me.

Cecelia blinked.

Let's go home, I said.

Did you bring the skunk book? she asked.

I explained that I'd had to return it to the library. She nodded. Good. That meant she could check it out herself, the next time she went. We walked back hand in hand, practicing pronouncing "crepuscular." Crep-us-Q-lar.

At night I lay awake. It was the time of night for imagining what your maid of honor might say in a speech, in the future. As a child I'd never drawn crayon sketches of poofy dresses or marched up and down with a pillowcase draped over my head. But I imagined my wedding. The important people in my life would lift a glass and tell a story. Whatever the story was, the wedding would be the epilogue.

The problem was that a maid of honor couldn't tell the story of Eli without making me look pathetic. *Isabel was in love with Eli for years. She moved back to town to pursue him, instead of to Philadelphia to pursue a career in natural science museum curation.*

In my heart of hearts, I thought it was better to move across the country for someone you weren't involved with than for someone you were. Then you weren't deluding yourself. You knew from the start it was a fantasy— no need to wait for the breakup to feel like an idiot. I doubted the crowd at my wedding would understand this reasoning.

A maid of honor was meant to embarrass you, of course. Once, she would opine, so-and-so was outlandishly drunk. But I wasn't drunk. I'd been in full control of all mental faculties when I agreed to house-sit for Jan and Steve.

I rolled over in bed. I reached out one index finger and touched the wall in front of my face. The paint was "eggshell." I thought that was the word. It wasn't "matte." Sometimes the bones of the house settled and something would creak. How lucky houses were—they could exist without action. No one expected them to *do* anything.

The house-sitting idea had shown up in a text from Brigitte. She'd been wondering what I wanted for a graduation present. And oh, while she was thinking of it, Jan was looking for a house sitter this summer. Three months. Any chance . . . ?

It had been spring. That was the season we all developed an interest in real estate. We sat in the library with one tab open to the weather forecast, one tab open to the essay we were writing, and three tabs open to apartment websites. We typed "Philadelphia" into the search bar as filler. It seemed the sort of thing. It wasn't New York; it wasn't far off. Someone had told us—somewhere we had read—it was more affordable. It had Young People.

In the evenings we propped a laptop on the porch railing and watched *House Hunters*.

Brigitte's text had the allure of the concrete. I'd been inside Jan's house before, so there was no need to account for fish-eye lenses. And it would give me time. I could figure out real jobs and real apartments when I wasn't worrying about essays. For a second, I pulled ahead in whatever race Mikayla and Henry and I were racing. I knew where I was going.

A breeze slipped through the screen of the open window. I rolled over again to face it. The moon must have been full, or a couple of calendar squares away from full. My jeans lay in a pile on the floor. They had the look of a mountain range seen from an airplane window. I hadn't been on an airplane in a long time, not since the clouds could speak. *Come*, the clouds used to say, *it's time to make snow angels.*

A skunk came over the mountain and Mikayla, in a purple dress, said, *Isabel was always weird about Eli*, and I was asleep.

Roger was the most popular yoga teacher. He was a person you met gradually. He'd shaken my hand on my first day, inclining his bald head as he pronounced it a pleasure to meet me. He was stout and wiry. Everything that bore noticing about him required a point of comparison. That first day, I couldn't have said his classes were popular, because I didn't know how many students the other classes had. I couldn't have known that the cluster of gray-haired women waiting to speak with him after class was unusual. He was a man, and the other instructors were women.

In late June, he paused while putting on his raincoat to ask how I was liking the job. His raincoat was plain and black and ended at his hips, just like mine. The last of the students finally trickled out. While they'd stood talking to Roger next to the stereo system in the studio, I'd refilled the bathroom paper towels, printed the daily transaction report, and powered down the computer and copy machine. Now I was waiting to lock the door behind us. Rain thrummed against the windows. I said it was an interesting job to have because I didn't know anything about yoga. Everything I saw became an observation.

Roger nodded. And what have you observed? he asked.

I locked the door. Now we were in the vestibule between the studio, the attorney's office it shared a building with, and the door to the outside. I took my umbrella out of my bag but didn't undo the Velcro around it.

The women really like to ask you questions, I said, facing the outer door as if we were still moving, even though we'd stopped. They don't do that with the other teachers—hang around after class to talk.

Roger tilted his head up, as if studying the drips lined up at the edge of the awning outside. Hmm, he said. That *is* an observation.

I mean they're flirting with you, I said after a moment. The silence of taciturn men could be uniquely frustrating and often led me to spurts of bravery.

Roger looked amused, in profile. Oh, he said, I understood that that was your interpretation.

A crack of thunder rolled down the street.

It's not yours?

He shrugged, pulling his hood up over his bald head. I couldn't imagine referring to Roger's head without putting the word "bald" in front of it. He was so bald. He probably massaged expensive vegan moisturizer into his scalp every night.

I think, he said, that women of a certain age just want someone to talk to, sometimes.

He let that sink in, then asked if I had a ride home—it was awfully wet out there. His wife was on her way to get him, and he was sure they could drive me, too, if I needed.

I shook my head quickly. Outside, I pinched the neck of my coat tighter around my chin. I'd misinterpreted the interaction—he'd been waiting for his wife, not for my conversation. What age, exactly, qualified one as a "woman of a certain age"? The phrase offended me, but I couldn't say why. Didn't everyone want someone to talk to? Was this desire something else I was meant to be embarrassed about? Or maybe it was more complicated— maybe it only became embarrassing once you reached the "certain age." Judy and I could talk with impunity because we were too young and too old. Also because we were talking to each other instead of to a man.

The Eldest Skunk had more conversations with the oriole. The compost smelled of tapioca, and then of apple cores.

He told her about three goats who wanted to cross a bridge, and taught her to count.

"See the leaves on the clover?" he said. "One, two, three. See the pigs in the story? Straw, sticks, stones. One, two, three."

The Eldest Skunk brought the oriole three underripe blueberries the next morning. Three was the number that fit in her mouth: one in each cheek and one under her tongue. She spat the berries carefully onto the ground at the base of the apple tree. Overjoyed, the oriole thought she was ready for bigger numbers. They waddled and flew together from dandelion to dandelion. One! Two! Three! Four, five, six, seven! Eight, nine, ten, eleven!

The Eldest Skunk only remembered "eleven." It tasted best to her ears.

The next time I went to Cecelia's house, the carpet was covered in skunk books. Her house didn't have a mudroom, so it was especially jarring. The door spat you right into the open-plan living room/kitchen. There were books all over the floor.

In the books, skunks learned to say please and threw each other surprise birthday parties. They dug for beetles. They walked by colored "Did you know?" boxes. Did you know a newborn skunk weighs the same as ten marshmallows?

We stayed inside because it was raining. Jon cleaned out the fridge. His earphones were in his back pocket instead of around his neck. He was supposed to be working whenever I was with Cecelia, but often spent time with the fridge—cleaning, excavating, procrastinating. Today he attached a piece of masking tape to a shelf on the door. MUSTARD. A pile of half-finished applesauce pouches lay behind him on the counter.

A skunk phase is better than a princess phase, he said.

I had a flashback to my high school history teacher proclaiming that sixty seconds was the maximum amount of time anyone really needed in the shower. It wasn't that I disagreed. Still, the teacher's hair had always been short enough not to need shampoo.

We kept getting only halfway through a book before Cecelia would decide we were done, push it shut, and put a different one in my lap. I worried I was enabling a quitter attitude. I went along with it anyway. Maybe being a quitter was a good thing—maybe it meant Cecelia would know how to change course when things weren't working.

I want to see a *real* skunk, she said.

In my head, I agreed. Out loud, I tried to explain that skunks didn't work like that. They appeared or they didn't. They were shy. If we wanted them too badly, they would never come.

Cecelia understood faster than I expected. Like Santa? she asked. He'll only bring the presents if you fall asleep?

At Jon and Amelie's, every Christmas Eve, they set out a plate of cookies. In the morning the cookies were gone, replaced with presents and a short note from Santa. What did skunks eat, Cecelia wanted to know? I pointed to a page in a National Geographic Kids book. Insects, larvae, eggs, small animals.

But what do they eat for dessert?

Jon, as the final arbiter of all knowledge, was consulted. Now there was a half-made sandwich on the counter, with a bottle of honey-mustard dressing and a jar of Dijon beside it.

Cecelia tugged on his pant leg. What do skunks eat for dessert?

Mustard, darling, said Jon without looking down.

Cecelia wanted to have Skunk Christmas right away. She would cover a plate in mustard and leave it on the stoop. In the morning there would be an empty plate.

By this point, Jon's brain had caught up to what was happening. You could see the battle playing out across his forehead. His eyebrows jumped together and apart. On the one hand, the danger of stifling his daughter's creativity. On the other hand, the waste of mustard!

But Cecelia, I said, don't you think Skunk Christmas should be a specific day? How will the skunks know to come looking for the mustard?

I suggested June 30—the eve of July 1. The switch between months was a good time for holidays. The skunks would know to expect special happenings.

Jon's eyebrows threw a "thank you" at me. June 30 was days and days away. It belonged to the future, and was likely to be forgotten.

Great idea, he said. That way, you'll have more time to prepare.

One twilight, the oriole had bad news. He valued his conversations with the Eldest Skunk, but his mate would be arriving soon. He and the skunk could still talk, but not as they once had. He would be busier. He would have duties.

The skunk understood, and didn't understand. She understood that he would be busy. She didn't understand why the busyness was bad news. To her, each hour of waking was measured by how hungry or cold she was at the time. Her desires were confined to the achievable. She never wished for sun when it was raining, though she might wish for a dry, hollow log.

She walked toward the stream. The oriole followed. He hadn't met his mate for this year, but he would know them when he saw them.

The Eldest Skunk wanted to show him the skunks in the water. Today only one water-skunk appeared. It didn't blink, even when a water strider skied over its eyebrow. The Eldest Skunk felt happy to be introducing her friends to each other.

The oriole dipped a toe in the stream. He turned his beak back and forth between the skunk in the water and the skunk on the land.

"Haven't you ever heard of a reflection?" he asked.

The Eldest Skunk made a paw print in the mud, and then another one next to it with the same paw. She looked at the skunk in the water with what could only be described as love.

The oriole stepped back.

"Never mind," he said. "Thank you for introducing me."

June 30 approached, and Cecelia did not forget. The skunks grew in her mind like an inflatable bouncy house, or a crush on a bespectacled stranger in a café.

I pushed her on the swings. She described what she would be for Halloween.

I'm going to be a skunk, she said.

With four-year-olds, the question of what to be for Halloween was never out of season. It was important to always have an answer ready, even if you would end up being something entirely different come October.

Cecelia wanted to wear all black. Amelie would glue white felt down her back. There would be a big fluffy tail—materials TBD. In one hand she would carry a jar of mustard, and in the other a spray bottle.

Today, the back of her T-shirt was covered in smiling butterflies. Her ribs, every time I gave her a push, felt more like plastic straws than bones.

But I'm going to be a nice skunk, she said, so I'm going to spray lavender-smell. Higher, Isabel, push me higher!

She wanted me to do an underdog. The word "underdog" hit me in the face, like so many things I'd forgotten.

My dad had done underdogs for me. An underdog was when you kept moving forward as you pushed the swing, and walked under it, lifting the child above your head before letting them swing down behind you. It was simple in memory. I gripped the sides of the swing and walked forward. Suddenly the physics didn't make any sense. I backed up. I tried again and the same thing happened.

I'm sorry, I said, I can't. You're going to fall out of the swing.

Cecelia kicked her legs impatiently. No, I'm not!

Then my arms aren't strong enough. I can't lift you that high.

She tilted her head back to look up at me. Daddy does underdogs all the time.

I know, I said. I'm sorry.

Cecelia squirmed off the swing and kicked some wood chips out of her sandals. Let's go back inside, she said.

Inside, we got right down to business. We had to finish our skunk holiday cards. The yellow crayon was already shorter than its siblings. We'd drawn so many mustard bottles. When we'd started the cards, Cecelia had wanted to draw the skunks themselves. But black and white was hard. She didn't understand how to let blank space be a color. She didn't understand why the white crayon, layered on top of the black one, only made things a muddy gray. Mustard bottles were easier. They were yellow. They could be outlined by me and colored in by her.

After cards were decorated, there was the problem of what to put inside. I refused to write "Merry Christmas." This was *Skunk* Christmas, I insisted. We were inventing the wheel. I didn't use that expression. Cecelia wouldn't have understood.

She rolled around on the carpet a bit, like she always did when grown-ups wanted her to be creative. Happy mustard, she said. Write that.

I wrote *Happy mustard.*

When Amelie got home from work, she sat cross-legged on the floor and read through every card. *Happy mustard. Wishing you a mustardy year to come. Stars and stripy skunks forever. I odor you! Dear Skunk, stop following me, love, the man in the book. Dear Skunk, I'm sorry, please come back, love, the man in the book. Dear Skunks, I love you a lot and would like to meet you but if you are too shy that's OK too, love, Cecelia.*

The oriole made his house out of sticks, and dead grasses, and strands of human hair that someone had plucked from their hairbrush and tossed out the bathroom window. The Eldest Skunk kept track of the nest. She looked up at it on her way to the compost bin, and again when she walked back from the compost bin.

The oriole didn't have time to dwell on his true love, the apple tree, anymore. He still dwelled *in* it. His brain was clogged with architectural mud, and mental maps of which stretches of ground held the tenderest earthworms, best suited to an infant oriole's gullet.

Did he love the apple tree less because he thought of it less often? No. But how else should we measure emotion?

Sometimes I woke in the middle of the night with the weight of a small mammal on my chest. I tried not to move. If Athena noticed me stirring, she would disappear.

In the linen closet there was a shelf for bath mats. Right above them was a shelf for smaller towels: hand towels on the left, washcloths on the right. The washcloths were all folded in quarters. Their corners matched up exactly in the stack. Sometimes I wondered if the closet had had a makeover before Jan and Steve left, or if it was naturally beautiful. Sometimes Athena was nowhere to be found. At those times, she was napping on the bath mats.

Finally I removed the bath mats, hand towels, and washcloths from the closet. The top bath mat was matted with cat hair. You could peel off sections of hair all in one piece, like Band-Aids. I put that one in the laundry basket.

Athena appeared at the top of the stairs. She sat down and looked at me, letting her tail drape over the first step. The tail swung back and forth.

I put the remaining bath mats on the shelf where the hand towels and washcloths had been, and vice versa.

Leaving the closet door open, I backed down the hall and sat on the carpet. Now the closet was between Athena and me.

Athena turned and trotted back down the stairs. Her belly swung back and forth underneath her. Her tail stood straight aloft.

So Cecelia had a purpose, and I had nothing. I lay on the couch and touched my phone screen.

At Cecelia's house, *Cinder Edna* lay forgotten under the coffee table. The first page was folded back under the cover by mistake, developing a crease that would one day rip half the words away. I tried to feel like a good influence, instead of like a math professor realizing their student has developed a more innate understanding of calculus than they could ever aspire to.

I clicked into "Messages." My conversation with Eli was just out of sight. If I scrolled down even a centimeter, it would appear—his name, and the *lit* that was still our last message—there beneath the text from Brigitte about whether or not I was interested in an armchair that had been posted in her "buy nothing" internet forum. In an effort to reuse, people sent out photos of things they didn't want anymore in case anyone else wanted them. I'd once arrived at my father's house to find Brigitte taking a picture of a mostly empty jar with a few Brazil nuts at the bottom. Originally it had been full of "mixed nuts," but it turned out Brigitte didn't like Brazil nuts.

She posted the picture. Later that afternoon a stranger came and picked up the almost empty jar.

I clicked into the message with Brigitte. It was a nice armchair—blue with fat buttons across the back. In those days there was something sinister about offers of furniture. They seemed designed to remind me that I had nowhere to put it.

I closed the app, then reopened it, scrolled to the message with Eli, and typed:

Hey, wondering if you'd want to get coffee on Tuesday?

I hit send without considering the implications of different punctuations or days of the week. Then I put my phone face down in the middle of the living room carpet. These moments of freedom, when I was so proud of myself for sending a message that I couldn't care at all about the reply, never got old. Sometimes they lasted until the next morning.

I folded laundry. I didn't turn on the radio.

On the evening of June 30, Jon texted me a bird's-eye-view photo of a plate of mustard on their porch steps. A moment later, another photo came in: Amelie holding a dish of crackers and a wine bottle.

Skunk Christmas, he said, with the little green checkmark emoji.

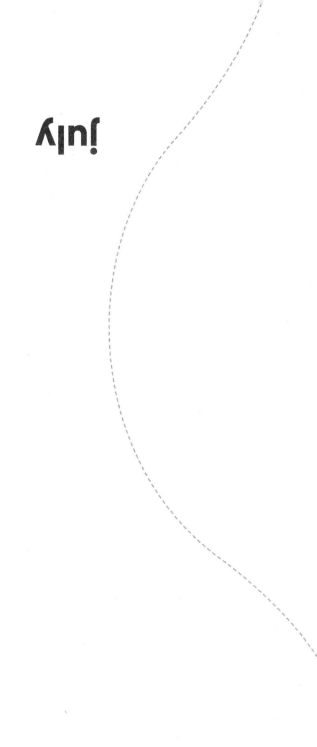

july

Eli said yes to Tuesday. I asked which café he wanted to go to. He said the Black Sheep. He said it had the best coffee in town. I closed and reopened the messages app before responding. It annoyed me—this implication that I didn't know where the best coffee was. I had grown up here!

At the same time, I couldn't tell if the houses on Elm Street had looked newer five years ago, or if college had turned me into a person who noticed peeling paint.

On Tuesday, I put on a tank top with buttons down the front. Then I took it off. I didn't know if I wanted the power of looking beautiful or the power of looking like I didn't care about beauty. Either way I couldn't wear sleeves. Underarm sweat spots could never be construed as power.

So that I wouldn't be early, I spent time printing out two poems from the internet. I taped them to Jan and Steve's fridge. I read them out loud. In the empty kitchen my voice sounded like a dried-out gel pen. One poem was by Robert Lowell and one was by Seamus Heaney. They were both about skunks. Robert Lowell's skunks were militaristic garbage swillers. I liked to read poetry by men that was inaccurate. It made me feel feminist. Seamus Heaney's poem was more true. It was more about a woman than it was about a skunk.

When I got to the café, Eli was already there. Usually, I arrived places first. It was a relief to not have to wait. It also made me feel severed from my personality.

He was wearing a T-shirt that said ACADIA NATIONAL PARK and had already ordered. I waited in line by myself.

When I sat down across from him, he asked what I'd gotten. He'd taken the booth seat. He could look out at the rest of the room, whereas I could only look at him.

Just coffee, I said.

Just black?

Yeah.

Eli had gotten an oat milk latte. We had the conversation about milk types. It was a conversation I often had with acquaintances—dairy versus plant-based, whole versus skim, oat versus almond. Once Eli had taken an internet quiz that was supposed to say what kind of milk you were. The quiz said he was pumpkin seed milk. Now, whenever he went to a new grocery store he asked if they had pumpkin seed milk. They never did. He still didn't know what he tasted like.

His eyes kept floating up to a spot above my right shoulder. I wondered if there was a print of one of his favorite paintings on the wall, or if an ex-girlfriend had walked in. Eventually I turned in my seat to look. It felt rude to be pointing out his rudeness.

Sorry, sorry, said Eli. It's my friend Rachid—he's the one working the espresso machine.

The man at the espresso machine wore a T-shirt with the sleeves cut off. Every time he twisted the portafilter on and off the machine, his shoulders flexed. I remembered that he liked to play tennis. He had a recently shampooed look about him that was different from the boys I'd known in college. So: Rachid had been here the whole time, watching or not watching. Had Eli known, when we arranged this coffee, that Rachid would be on shift? If Eli and Rachid were girls, I wouldn't have needed to wonder. The answer would have been yes.

I asked when Rachid got off, and if we should invite him to join us, but Eli said not for another few hours. I asked if Rachid working there meant Eli got free coffee. Eli shrugged.

In a way, Rachid's presence was another relief. It gave a physical reality to the feeling that everything was happening somewhere over my head.

Do you like living here? I asked. Being back?

He shrugged. I do. It's a good place. Honestly there's a lot of young people—people I'd never met.

I nodded.

And like, I saw Mrs. Leopold at the dentist the other day.

I took a sip of coffee. I liked that he saw running into your old calculus teacher at the dentist as a positive. It was relaxing to be in a place where people had already made up their minds about you. Your current actions had little bearing on your image. In high school I never drank black coffee. In high school I went to this café a lot.

Will you stay here? Eli rolled his paper napkin between his fingers.

I shrugged.

I know, I know, said Eli, shaking his head. Terrible question.

No, it's a good question, I said. I just don't know the answer.

What's your alternative? Like, is it here or anywhere, or here or New York?

Philadelphia. Is where I was going to go.

Mikayla was in Philadelphia, and Henry. Orin had run away to Europe. Sometimes he posted ominous statistics about climate change in the rectangle of his Instagram story.

But . . . ? Eli wiggled his fingers in the silence like a fill-in-the-blank.

I tried to take another sip of coffee, but my cup was already empty. I wished I understood my own motivations. If I had, I would have explained them to him. Something about Eli always made me want to scoop out my tonsils and hand them to him on a paper towel.

At one point he knocked over the last tablespoon of his latte and we had to get more napkins. Did him knocking over his drink mean he was nervous? I never knew what made for a good date—free-flowing conversation or being so attracted to someone that you couldn't speak. I never knew if it was attraction that made me unable to speak. This wasn't a date.

The second time I saw the skunks, there was only one. The ankles of my sweatpants were bunched around my thighs from sleep.

I'd been having a dream about a grocery store that was also an art museum. In the dream, Eli had been there. It's a commentary on consumerism, he kept saying. We expect our food to be art. The price of art is going down because we demand that everything be art. He was carrying our basket and I kept adding things to it, things I knew we didn't need, just to make our hands bump into each other. A jar of pickled beets. A roll of paper towels. I decided I wanted a different brand of paper towels because our hands hadn't touched the first time. In produce, Eli said the apples were obeying the rule of thirds. Could Eli tell I didn't know what the rule of thirds was? That they were equal—Granny Smiths, Pink Ladies, Golden Delicious—felt too simple. I didn't understand why it was a bad thing for the price of art to be falling. On the museum steps I lost him in the crowd. Then the steps were empty. He was at the bottom and I was at the top and we were running toward each other. It was always you, he said. It was a good kiss. The steps turned out to be a grocery store pyramid of apples. There were apples thundering down all around us and it was a good kiss.

I rolled over in bed and lifted the corner of the blinds. It was raining. The raindrops made an extra window screen between me and the world. The skunk, down below in the grass, was a drenched pilgrim. Nothing could shift or hasten her route.

By the time I got downstairs she was gone. When had I decided it was a she? I circled the house in my rain jacket. The earthworms made long straight lines on the driveway.

I made a cup of instant coffee and sat at the table, stirring. Next to the coffee was a blank sheet of paper. *Dear Skunks*, I wrote. Then I got stuck. What was there to say about the skunks? Of course there was the smell—the spraying. Everyone's mind jumped to the spraying. I often forgot about the spraying entirely, which was nice because it made me feel that I wasn't like other people.

The picture book hadn't mentioned the smell. The threat of the smell was so obvious it didn't need to be named. The man was wary of the skunk from the start.

I felt sorry for the skunks. Their cultural identity was subsumed by a single action. How were they to know if an approaching creature was looking for genuine connection, or only courting danger? And once it happened, everyone forgot about the skunk. Everyone ran shrieking to take a shower and tell their friends. Evolutionarily, this must have been the point—the skunk was free to escape. But it made me sad. How did the skunk feel after? Triumphant? Exhausted? Did reactions vary, or did it mostly feel the same for every skunk, every time?

I had too many questions, or too many ways of phrasing the same question. Was a skunk's first spray a rite of passage? Was it something adolescent skunks looked forward to, or dreaded? Or did skunk culture send them so many mixed messages they didn't know what to feel?

The piece of paper went in the recycling. It wasn't what I meant at all. I wanted to know if the skunk was lonely or just alone.

I lay on the couch again and touched my phone. I clicked into "Messages." This time my conversation with Eli was right there on the first screen. I didn't have to scroll down to be reminded. The last message was still my *me too!* in response to his *hey thanks for the coffee idea, had a great time*. I stared at the words. Eli's message attributed the "coffee idea" to me. Was that accurate, I wondered? Yes, I had been the one to text him asking about coffee. In academia that was how you owned something—by writing it down. But Eli had been the one to say the idea out loud, before that, in the kitchen of his childhood home. Maybe he'd forgotten. Maybe he hadn't considered it his idea because he hadn't meant it.

With dates, a follow-up text was supposed to include a "we should do this again sometime," even if you had no intention of seeing the other person again, ever. It was common courtesy. But my coffee with Eli hadn't been a date. In a way, the lack of "we should do this again sometime" was encouraging. It gave me fewer opportunities to doubt his sincerity.

Since I had sent the text initiating the coffee, it was up to him to send a text initiating something else. I wondered if he felt that since my *me too!* hadn't left much room for the conversation to be continued, the responsibility for reinitiation was actually mine. Or, if he did remember that the coffee idea had been his, maybe he felt that I should have the next idea. Was he a person who enjoyed texting for texting's sake, or did he only text as a way of facilitating in-person interactions?

I clicked into Instagram and navigated to the profile for the bakery he worked at. The latest post said it was strawberry rhubarb season. They would have strawberry rhubarb bars, while supplies lasted. Hashtag, come and get it. Hashtag, local produce. Eli clearly wasn't in charge of their social media.

The couch cushions kept sliding forward. They threatened to dive to the floor, dumping me into the underneath with all the lost pencils and crumbs. I had grown up with a futon. The shifting cushions were unfamiliar and disconcerting.

My phone often made me unhappy. I knew it wasn't really the phone's fault—it was what was inside the phone, combined with what was inside me. I closed Instagram and checked my email. No new messages. I opened Instagram again. I couldn't think of any reason to put my phone down. Eventually I clicked into YouTube and watched videos of skunks. Skunk videos were sort of like porn in that once you thought you understood what the internet had to offer, you could add another search term, sort of at random—stuck, kitchen, in the rain—and be confronted with a whole new dimension of videos. Skunks, it turned out, often got their heads stuck in jars. They'd be trying to lick up what the humans had left behind, and then they'd be stuck. In the videos, they swung their jar-heads back and forth in wide arcs, like time-lapse sunflowers following the sun throughout the course of a day. The head-swinging did little to dislodge the jars. One local TV station in Ohio had done a news story about a stuck skunk. The jar in this instance was a family-sized container of Skippy peanut butter. There was a lot of footage from before the animal control agent arrived. I wondered who had been called first—the rescuer or the people with the video cameras. Had the journalists asked the animal control agent to hold off until they got the right angle? Had the skunk known it was being filmed?

I would visit Eli at the bakery, I decided. It would be a coincidence, since social media was still the only reason I knew about his job. Any knowledge gleaned from social media—even if you hadn't sought it out—had to be denied. I would go after work the next day. I was an adult! I had a job! A baked good could be a reward as well as a coincidence.

In one rectangle, Henry stands over a fallen pizza box in the dark, hands clasped to his cheeks. The flash makes his eyes into little silver sink drains. The pizza is blurry. The slices drape over the edge of the box, slack and soggy, half on the cardboard and half on the sidewalk.

A few days later, Henry's hands slice a fresh loaf of focaccia. The steam appears like smoke on the screen. Halved cherry tomatoes dot the top of the bread.

A poster on a bus, zoomed in enough to be slightly grainy, advertises an opportunity: POOP FOR SCIENCE. Researchers hope to cure a disease. Participants will be paid up to forty dollars per poop.

The sun sets over tall buildings.

Henry and a stranger run up the museum steps, the ones everyone runs up when they're reenacting that scene from that movie. In the background audio, Mikayla laughs.

An album cover on a black background. It's an album Henry liked, that he claimed reminded him of me—the fourth track, anyway. I never liked it. All the lyrics, not just the lyrics of the fourth track, had too much in common with Hallmark cards. That Henry related to them wasn't encouraging. It proved he was more in love with the concept of a relationship than with me personally, but of course he got mad when I said that.

The sun sets, again, over tall buildings.

I pushed my bike down the street, one pedal banging into my ankles. The bakery was a couple of blocks from the yoga studio, and you weren't supposed to bike on the downtown sidewalks. I'd biked to work. A little girl balanced on the curb between the concrete and the grass in front of a church. She put one sparkly plastic shoe in front of the other, holding on to her father's hand. This is *my* sidewalk, she said to him as I passed. That's *your* sidewalk.

Maybe, I thought, I would buy a croissant.

The bakery was out of croissants. There was an empty wicker basket in the display case, with a laminated sign that said CROISSANTS. The basket wasn't really empty—it held crumbs and wax paper.

And the person behind the counter was a woman, not an Eli. She had long curly red hair. The hair set me against her. It was exactly the sort of hair I had wanted for myself as a child.

You're out of croissants? I asked.

She nodded.

Obviously they were out of croissants. I hadn't learned anything by asking, only revealed myself as a customer prone to living in denial.

The bakery had four round tables for sitting and eating at. None of them were occupied. Next to the register sat a bowl of donut holes. When I was little and too small to see over the counter, my dad had bought me these donut holes. I couldn't remember what they tasted like. I used to eat them in small bites. After every bite I would lick my fingers. Then my fingers would be damp and more sugar would stick to them. It had been like trying to clean the sand off your feet at the beach, except pleasurable. Once I'd asked to buy an extra donut hole, to feed to the chipmunk we sometimes saw outside the bakery. My dad had said chipmunks didn't like donut holes and I had believed him.

The red-haired woman straightened a stack of wax paper bags. I could tell she was trying not to make me feel self-conscious about how long it was taking me to pick a baked good. Part of me wanted a donut hole and part of me was scared. Even though I couldn't remember what they tasted like, what if they tasted different from before?

The water cooler in the corner gurgled.

I bought an oatmeal raisin cookie and left.

Outside, Eli was locking his bike to the bike rack. His bike was red and had those handlebars that curved under. My handlebars stuck straight out to the sides. From this I understood that I was the less serious biker.

Isabel! he said.

Oh, I said, hi! I didn't need to pretend to be surprised. I was actually surprised.

He said he worked at the bakery. He asked what I had gotten.

I held open the wax paper bag and he leaned in to look. There was a small hole in the fabric of his T-shirt right next to the neckline.

Rookie mistake, he said. Not our best product. Not chewy enough, eye-em-oh.

What *is* your best product? I asked.

The donut holes.

I nodded a couple of times to take up space. He rocked his weight from the balls of his feet to his heels. He was on the brink of something.

Here, he said, come back in, I'll get you a donut hole. They're like, sixty-five cents. I mean, I'm allowed to give them away.

He held open the door of the bakery. I didn't see any option besides walking through the door. Even if there had been other options I would have walked through the door.

The red-haired woman seemed younger, now. When she saw Eli she exclaimed something about how a band had released a new album, and had he listened, and what did he think?

You're kidding, he said, swinging his backpack off as he went around the counter. This is Isabel, he said.

Until Eli pointed me out, it wasn't clear if Red-Haired Girl had registered my presence, or that I was the same person who had just taken too long to buy an oatmeal raisin cookie.

She's here for a donut hole, Eli explained, selecting one with a pair of tongs and dropping it onto a piece of wax paper. He slid the paper toward me across the counter.

Thanks, I said.

I took a small bite. Eli said no, what was I doing, a donut hole had to be eaten all in one bite, that was the point of it. Women, he sighed, rolling his eyes.

What the fuck, Eli, said Red-Haired Girl. That's so sexist.

Eli shrugged. He wrinkled his nose.

I'm Brynn, said the girl, turning to me. Don't listen to him.

My mouth was full of donut hole. I'd stuck the rest of it in my mouth as soon as Eli said it should be eaten in one bite. It was a disappointingly normal-sized bite. My jaw didn't have to open any wider than it usually did. Still, my mouth was full enough that I couldn't talk.

Brynn stared at me. God, Eli, she said. You're such a bad influence. I'm going to check on the baguettes.

She swept through a swinging door into the kitchen. She really walked like that: like sweeping.

I folded the wax paper into a little square. Thanks for the donut hole, I said.

It's nothing, he said. Don't worry about it.

I should go, I said. Good to see you, though. Athena says hi.

Eli laughed a little bark of a laugh, the kind that meant it was genuine. I had surprised him. I didn't know what was so surprising about a cat.

Well, he said. Tell Athena I say hi back.

Outside, I wasn't sure what to do with the cookie. I didn't see any chipmunks. Still, I tore off a corner and set it on the curb. Maybe the chipmunks were feeling shy.

The Eldest Skunk took a piece of dead grass between her teeth and pulled. It came away like a leg disengaging from a cricket. She carried it in her mouth to the stream, and tossed it gently to the skunk in the water. The skunk in the water looked at the dead grass. It hung between them. So the skunk in the water was confused, too, thought the Eldest Skunk.

She brought more pieces of dead grass and laid them in straight lines in the mud on the shore. Then she brought pieces of green grass, and live earthworms, and wood chips, and oblong pebbles that fit neatly beneath her tongue. The earthworms kept squirming out of order. She nosed them back. Hold still.

Soon she had a long line of short lines. The short lines ran perpendicular to the long one, railroad-track style rather than traffic-lane style. What good has a long line of short lines ever done anyone? The Eldest Skunk counted her trophies. One, two, three, eleven. One, two, three, eleven. Eventually she let the earthworms go. The sun was higher in the sky and it was time for bed. Under the forsythia, she braided her tail with her siblings' and dreamed of ants. In the dream, the ants were coming out of the hole at the top of their hill. Instead of marching down the hill headfirst, they lay perpendicular to the ground and rolled, enjoying the cylindrical properties of a thorax.

Her siblings giggled in their sleep.

But when they woke, the Eldest Skunk's confusion was still there. When had a twilight become connected to the dawn that preceded it? Why did the problems of one waking extend to the next?

The oriole might have said that this was purpose and direction, and he would have meant that this was what created a plot. But the oriole didn't say anything. He was down by the stream, taking advantage of an unlikely concentration of worms in the mud.

The Eldest Skunk kept thinking about building materials. The thoughts were inaccessible to her siblings because her siblings still hadn't heard about the pigs. The skunks had never been differentiated like this. It hurt. The Eldest Skunk was reminded of building materials more and more frequently. The bottom layer of grass, where last year's blades decomposed, seemed like straw. A forsythia bush was already a house of sticks. There were stones at the bottom of the stream.

So there was nowhere for the thoughts to go because she couldn't share them. They built up inside her like so many leg hairs in a shower drain. She tripped over her siblings' tails, either because she needed to feel closer to them or because she wasn't focused on the present. Never mind that solving the second problem might have solved the first. Her siblings got tired of the bruises on their tails, and the Eldest Skunk spent more time by herself.

This was the state of things when the oriole came to say goodbye. If he hadn't become a father, he might have known it was his fault. If he hadn't become a father, he might have been curious about what would happen next. That day, the compost smelled of kale gone slimy at the edges.

"Goodbye," said the oriole. He was a father, now. His children had grown up, except the one that had died. First they'd hatched, then they'd eaten as many worms as he could regurgitate, and then they'd eaten as many worms as he could carry whole. Now their childhood was over. It was time for him to go.

The Eldest Skunk swished her tail from left to right, tracing an invisible rainbow in the air above her haunches. Then she brought her tail back to the left, keeping it low to the ground, and repeated the original swish.

It could only be solved with motion. When a playground swing changes direction, there is a moment of stillness between rising and falling. Something like that was happening inside the Eldest Skunk. The potential energy was building up, and could only go away by becoming kinetic.

What was her fortune? She needed to see more things in case she would know her fortune when she saw it.

The oriole had caused the disquiet. He'd been a pair of eyes, and the skunk had seen herself through those eyes, walking back and forth across the same stretch of grass. An oriole couldn't see that grass existed in layers. From up above, it was all green. Yes, he came down to eat the beetles sometimes. No, he did not pay attention. It's not that he was unobservant, only that he was focused on the sky instead of the grass.

So the Eldest Skunk had to leave. At twilight she made a big pile of acorn caps under the forsythia and slipped away.

My father and I went wild blackberry picking. We met at 8:30 AM and drove together into the hills, leaving my car at his house. It was early in the season. Blackberries shouldn't have been ripe yet, but Brigitte said these ones would be. It was her secret picking spot. She gave us directions. The berries there were always fatter and juicier than anywhere else, she said.

I buckled my seat belt and my father handed me an Oreo. Breakfast of champions.

In the car I rested my head against the window. It could have been seven years ago. He could have been driving me to school. Parallel to the road, a rock wall ran through the woods. Each section looked the same as the last, but if you tried to focus on a single stone, the illusion fell apart: the car was moving very fast.

My father had seen a coyote the day before. He was due for another planting of salad greens, and Brigitte wanted him to fix the shelf in the pantry.

We laughed about Cecelia wanting to be a skunk for Halloween. We hoped it would last, and that her friends would understand how cool she was. Next year the streets could be flooded with children, all wielding lavender-scented spray bottles.

Cecelia's family had gone to Maine for most of July. I would miss them.

The trees around the blackberry patch hung heavy with wild grapevines, which in turn hung heavy with dew. Water droplets shook down on us as we squeezed between branches, holding the longer twigs out of the way for each other. I was soaked within minutes.

Brigitte had stayed home to make the pie dough. It was because her knee was acting up, not because she was a woman. My father and I carried yellow plastic buckets.

Hear that? he said, pausing with a twig held between forefinger and thumb. Pileated woodpecker.

We listened. The call was a sarcastic laugh or a sharp chiding.

The berries were real blackberries, not black raspberries. Most people didn't know the difference. Black raspberries are small and hollow, thimble shaped. True blackberries are solid, and have polyps the size of engorged ticks. In preschool I'd argued with my friends about the contents of their lunches. No, I remembered crying, those *aren't* blackberries.

Thorns gripped the thighs of my jeans. In the evening there would be faint red lines across my skin, as if Athena had been sitting on my lap. Denim only did so much. I lifted leaves to see if there was anything underneath. It was like one of Cecelia's lift-the-flap books. If the berries had any hint of maroon, I passed onward. They needed to be truly black, truly ripe. They needed to fall, salivating, into my palm, their softness toeing the line between luxury and revulsion. Some of them were stunted or mottled. I was more squeamish than my father, but I picked according to his standards rather than my own. I'd studied these standards from a young age, learning to push down my natural instincts. An ugly berry could still be edible, and shouldn't be wasted.

The berries thudded into the bucket. My father was out of sight behind a stand of adolescent birches. I could hear when he'd covered the bottom of his bucket because the thuds turned muted, like in that children's book *Blueberries for Sal*. In my own bucket, large patches of plastic still showed through. The plastic was a relief. As a child, I'd felt ashamed of picking slower. I'd thought growing up would mean keeping up. Now I felt afraid to outpace him. I wasn't tall enough for my father to be shrinking.

We didn't need so many berries for the pie. We would freeze most of them. It would be a peach-blackberry pie, and Brigitte had bought the peaches at a farm stand the day before. I kept wading through the brambles. The sun rose. As the dew dried, sweat took its place, and my shirt stayed damp. I ate one of the berries. It squidged against my tongue. I ate another. This one was more bitter, and the bitterness was pleasant, too.

Two robins argued in a pine tree above us, and three perfect berries eyed me from behind a spiderweb. I was so lucky. Each strand of spiderweb stood out against the morning light. The spider wasn't home. Had it had a late night, or was it lying in wait, ready to pounce on unsuspecting insects? Maybe there wasn't any conflict. Maybe the robins were only having a conversation.

Should've worn gloves, said my dad, appearing again amid the trees. He held up his forearms. He wore a green long-sleeved T-shirt. His hands were stained brown and purple.

Most of it's juice, he said.

Meaning some of it was blood, from the thorns. He liked to gather and call it hunting.

On the drive back, we passed a church. Overflow cars dotted the side of the road. A sign out front spelled GOD WELCOMES U in movable letters.

Then my father said something he had said before, and would say again: If there is a God, I refuse to believe he wants me to spend a morning like this inside a building.

Then it was raining. Ellie and I had planned to go swimming. It wasn't pleasant puddle-stomping rain. It came cold and fat from the sky.

wanna sit in a cafe and pretend to be Italian grandfathers?

I smiled at my phone where it lay on the arm of Jan and Steve's couch. Ellie and I were thinking about plan Bs from our separate houses. Where did she get this shit? What did the word "Italian" mean in this context? It didn't have to do with Italy, but the sentence wouldn't have been the same without it.

I typed yes with lots of *S*'s, and my phone autocorrected it to yes with even more *S*'s.

Her next message said: *Black sheep?*

I didn't reply immediately. I wandered to the kitchen sink, where my dishes from breakfast sat unwashed. *meh*, I typed, then rolled up my sleeves and turned on the water. If we went to the Black Sheep, Rachid might be on shift. Would he remember me as the girl who had sat with Eli that one time? Had Eli said anything to Rachid about me, either before or after that one time? Going to the Black Sheep seemed like an unnecessary risk. It seemed like it might distract me from Ellie in a way that I would later be ashamed of.

Ellie's next suggestion was the bakery where Eli worked.

I moved the sponge across my cereal bowl in slow circles, watching the soap slither down my wrists. My phone screen, on the counter next to me, went dark and then lit up again: *actually yes their insta says they have this strawberry rhubarb bar on special this week. we must go.*

The cereal bowl was curved in a way that made it difficult to balance in the drain rack. I had to lean it up a few times to get it to stay. We had to go to the bakery. The only thing worse than doing something because of a guy was *not* doing something because of a guy.

I went upstairs and took a couple of shirts on and off. I settled on one with a line of three strawberries across the chest. It didn't fit me right. The shoulders were too small, making my actual shoulders look too big. That was okay. It made it clear that I cared more about dressing to theme—strawberry rhubarb—than looking good. My rain jacket went on over the strawberry shirt. I zipped it all the way to my chin and pulled up the hood. Rain was a theme, too.

I ran into Ellie a block from the bakery. We'd both parked on the side streets where you didn't have to pay.

Are you getting the strawberry rhubarb bar, too? she asked by way of greeting. She warned me that she wouldn't give me a bite. Her strawberry rhubarb bar was all hers. If I wanted any I had to get my own. But did I think they would heat it up for her if she asked? And would they do that in a microwave or a toaster oven? She didn't want it soggy. She wanted something warm and crisp.

I shrugged. You can always ask.

I held the door for her, and she walked past me into the shop, shaking rain from her jacket sleeves. Eli stood behind the counter.

Look what the cat dragged in! he said.

I tried to decide if he was pleased to see me, or only being good at customer service.

Ellie looked back at me, confused. She didn't know Eli. Why was this guy acting so familiar with random customers? I knew Eli from school, and Ellie had always been separate from that part of my life. She grew up one town over, in a different district. It was why it had been so easy to stay friends through college. We'd never relied on daily contact to glue us together. Our relationship was just us. Other people, and the shifting loyalties of school friend groups, couldn't get in the way.

I waved. Hey, Eli.

Oh! said Ellie, looking back and forth. You know each other! This is perfect. It makes me feel much better about how annoying a customer I'm about to be.

Ellie was good at acting at-home in situations. She explained to Eli that she needed to know the options for heating up a strawberry rhubarb bar. Could it be put in a toaster oven for a minute? Or the normal oven, if there wasn't a soufflé in there already that would be ruined by opening the door? The microwave, after all, would be unacceptable.

Uh, we don't make soufflés, said Eli. So, sure? Isabel, do you want one too?

No, no, I said. I'm still thinking.

Eli took a single strawberry rhubarb bar into the back room.

Ellie frowned at me, like, *remember I'm not giving you a bite.*

I widened my eyes back, like, *I know, I know.*

I didn't know what to get. A donut hole might be a nice nod to Eli, but it would look small and lonely next to Ellie's bar. I didn't want to seem like one of those girls who was frightened of eating. In the end I got the strawberry rhubarb bar and said I wanted it cold.

We sat at a small circle table in the corner. There was one other customer, an old man reading a newspaper. He held it up in front of him with two hands instead of laying it flat on the table. His hairstyle endeared him to me—it was the quintessential bald-on-top-with-ear-tufts. At what age had he started to bald? Partial baldness suited him well, now, but it couldn't always have been like that. Maybe one never stopped needing to grow into things.

Our strawberry rhubarb bars came on plates because we'd asked for them "for here." Ellie made me push my chair back so she could take a picture, holding her phone horizontal above the table. She shifted my plate slightly to the left, and hers slightly to the right. Diagonals were important in art, weren't they? She said maybe the next generation of iPhone would have a thermal camera. Then she could post one of the photos on Instagram and everyone would know how much cooler she was than me, because she'd gotten hers heated up.

Maybe, I agreed.

She went to grab forks from the napkin station by the register. Eli didn't look up. He sat on a stool, leaning his elbows on the counter, looking at something on his phone.

Finally, we had utensils, the photos were done, and we could take a bite. The virtue of the unheated bar was structural integrity. It held its shape on my fork. I found this comforting. It was like a pair of boots with good arch support, but for my mouth. There were lines that the world would stay inside of.

Ellie's fork dripped strawberry rhubarb goop. She closed her eyes while she chewed. We talked about her mother, and long versus short raincoats. Ellie used to find her mother's long raincoat horribly embarrassing. Now she just wanted something that would keep her butt dry if she sat on a wet bench.

At some point the bell on the door jingled. An adult with two children walked in. Ellie leaned forward across the table. Okay, she whispered, so how do you know the guy behind the counter?

I glanced at Eli. He was talking to the adult, gesturing at the display of breads behind him. The adult was nodding, trying to maintain eye contact while keeping the kids from sticking their noses against the glass of the display case.

Oh, I said, he's Jan and Steve's son. I tried to scrape up a crumb with my fork. The ones I'm house-sitting for?

Ellie nodded, looking over at the counter.

Don't stare, I said.

I'm not.

Still.

What's his name?

Eli.

Eli. She turned the word over in her mouth. Did he go to school with you?

I nodded. I knew why the name sounded familiar to her. I couldn't tell if I wanted her to remember it—the thing I could see her brain reaching toward.

He was one of the ultimate boys, I said.

Oh, right! she said. The hot ones! Maybe that's it.

My cheeks felt warm, though I knew Eli hadn't heard. He was right there.

But that was high school, I said. We're just, like, acquaintances now. Hardly even that.

Ellie took another big bite of strawberry rhubarb bar. To be fair, she said as she chewed, he's still hot.

•

I thought I had escaped. I hadn't.

Ellie called as I turned into Jan and Steve's driveway. I put her on speakerphone and her voice rustled through the parked car: Wait, wait, wait, she said. Wasn't Eli the one you hooked up with?

Technology had dulled the safety of distance. In the olden days, physical space could be counted on to impede communication; if you wanted to avoid someone, you only had to move across the country. Today, miles meant nothing. A few finger taps could always produce the outlines of a person: a voice, a face, a tweet about postmodern armchairs from last October.

I pressed my head back into the headrest. Ugh, I said, yeah.

Okay, said Ellie. Okay, hold on, I'm just getting home, I think my housemates are here. Wait while I walk through the living room. Don't hang up.

I unbuckled my seat belt and took off my raincoat, wadding it into a ball and hugging it against my body. Over the phone, doors opened and closed. Pleasantries were exchanged. One of the roommates wanted to order pizza for dinner. One of the roommates thought they'd been eating out too much.

A door shut on the other end of the line. Why didn't you *say* that? Ellie wanted to know.

There were lots of responses I could have given. The responses wouldn't have been lies, but I wouldn't have been confident they were true. I might have said I'd felt awkward talking about it within earshot of Eli. I might have said it was high school and didn't matter anymore. I might have said I thought Ellie didn't like it when I talked about boys.

And what was Ellie's motivation for the question? Was she hurt that I'd kept something from her?

I told her the hookup was a long time ago. It hadn't seemed relevant.

She sighed. I can't tell if you're being dumb on purpose.

What?

Hookups are always relevant.

We were both quiet for a minute, and then spoke at the same time.

Look, I have to go—

If you want to—

It's fine, it's fine, said Ellie. I'll see you later. You're just funny, sometimes.

After we hung up, I got out of the car and went into the house. I hung my raincoat in the mudroom closet next to Eli's parents' winter parkas.

It was too hot to turn on the stove. The rain had pinned the heat to the earth, and the air felt like waking up feverish and sweaty under a hotel room blanket. I chopped celery into three-inch logs and spread peanut butter down the center. In a cabinet, behind the turbinado sugar, I found a single-serving box of raisins. I placed raisins on the celeries one at a time, like I was dealing cards. It seemed important for each stalk to end up with an equal number.

Eli and I had hooked up in high school. He'd been a senior, and known. I'd been a sophomore, and unknown. There was no way to tell the story without arousing pity: I had been used for my body. Yet I still believed, as I had then, that I had used Eli more than Eli had used me. He'd been rewarded with mediocre sex and slight disapproval from a segment of his female friends. I'd become known.

I could never explain this to Ellie. If I said high school could be divided neatly into two pieces, Before Eli and After Eli, she would have shaken her head. She would have felt that she was a grown-up, while I was a child of the patriarchy. And maybe she would have been right. But what was I supposed to do about it? You couldn't choose your parents.

Every time I bit into a new stick of celery, I clamped my teeth around the unbroken fibers and turned my head from side to side, stripping them from the rest of the stalk. Celery was the vegetarian version of stringy meat. Dogs and babies found it comforting to gnaw on things.

In the past, I had tried to write a short story that began with the line *He was an eight and I was a mermaid*. It was going to be a story about Halloween costumes. It never went anywhere. In reality, Eli was a bass and I was an alto.

At our high school, the freshmen all had to do chorus, and they all had to be part of the big, non-auditioned freshman choir. After that year, chorus became optional, and you had to audition. My friends all auditioned, so I did, too. The choral director let all my friends in, so he let me in, too. "You know, Isabel," he said to me in his office, after I had sung the scale, "you're a good person. This chorus needs more good people." He went to church every Sunday, but he also believed in earthly rewards. So then I was in a chorus with Eli Homer-Drummond.

I'm putting the choral director's words in quotes because it's exactly what he said—everything else I don't trust memory to reproduce. The choral director meant he had problems getting theater kids to be quiet when he asked them to. He meant I didn't quite belong, so maybe I would be a good influence. I smiled and nodded.

He was naive. To think that in a room with Eli Homer-Drummond, I might be an influence!

The choral director felt passionately about vowels. We spent a lot of chorus with our mouths open. We massaged our jaws. We practiced tongue placement. It was the era of Snapchat, which was like texting with pictures instead of with words. In another world, Snapchat might have enhanced our understanding of poetic imagery. In this world, we snuck pictures of our friends and drew penises coming out of their mouths.

The upperclassmen cared about team spirit and group bonding. This made it difficult to analyze social interactions. Did they want to be friends, or were they just being inclusive? They started a group chat so we could plan an apple-picking trip, and also so the cream of the mouth-penis picture crop could be distributed more widely.

The group chat gave everyone access to everyone else's usernames. Once you knew someone's username, you could add them as a "friend." I added Damien. He was a sophomore tenor. No one talked about him, but he existed comfortably in multiple social spheres. He played the drums and did Model UN. In other words, he was a good candidate for a crush. People understood the appeal, but it wasn't outlandish to hope something might actually happen.

Damien added me back. Since I'd done the adding, I assumed it was up to him to send the first message. He didn't send anything. I complained about it to Claudia. Claudia was an alto, too.

Then Eli added me. I was in the doctor's office when it happened, sitting on the crinkly paper of the exam table. The nurse had already come and gone. I was waiting for the doctor to come press on my abdomen and ask if I felt any pain. My phone screen lit up. In the same way that our brains recognize words without looking at the individual letters, I understood what had happened. Eli's username was something like eliiiiiii14. There were more *i*'s than it made sense to count. It was lucky they had already taken my blood pressure.

I had to message Eli. It would have been hypocritical not to, after complaining about Damien not messaging me. I didn't want to be like my mother. I often accused my mother of hypocrisy. In the passenger seat on the way home, I held my phone at my belly button. I tucked my chin down so the skin folded and rolled. My friends and I called this a "thumb pic" because your head and neck blended together into one vaguely thumb-shaped column. I hit send. Even back then I believed in the power of looking bad on purpose.

Eli opened the picture but didn't reply. On Monday I asked Claudia if Eli had added her, too. He hadn't. But a story that's all "he sent this Snapchat, she sent that Snapchat" is no story at all.

Ellie says I asked her if she ever felt the pressure to leave. I don't remember asking but she says it happened. It wasn't at the bakery so it must have been on one of our walks. We would have been somewhere between the yarn store and the green house with the orange door. Across June and July, we did that walk maybe three times. Ellie loved a statement door. This one was deep within the network of residential streets behind the yarn store, and the yarn store was halfway between Ellie's apartment and Jan and Steve's.

Three was fewer walks than we'd expected to go on. It was what always happened when you suddenly lived close to someone you'd lived far away from. You expected to see them all the time, and then you hardly saw them at all. When they'd lived far away, they could be a priority. Living nearby made a person reschedulable.

I can imagine a few ways I might have said it.

Maybe we saw a hot air balloon and I said, Why do we expect young people to be like hot air balloons?

I would have said it knowing that Ellie would need an explanation, and then I would be able to say what I was really thinking. Ellie would have pointed out that a hot air balloon was not a good metaphor. Hot air balloons always came down relatively close to where they started. The point of a hot air balloon was not to leave, but to get a nice view of where you had been and would be.

Or maybe we were talking about capitalism. People knew bigger wasn't better, but they needed to *feel* that bigger wasn't better. And what about distance, I would have said, don't you think that's part of it? Don't you think we need to realize that getting farther away isn't better, either?

Ellie might have frowned. She might have thought I was talking about air travel. It was killing the planet. Everyone needed to take local vacations by public bus rather than flying off across the oceans.

But that wasn't what I meant at all. I meant to ask if she, too, worried that her continued existence in this town was perceived as a "failure to launch." And was there any truth in that perception? I was working in a yoga studio, and the people in Philadelphia were working in coffee shops. What made it more acceptable to flounder in a new place than in a place steeped with memories?

Maybe Ellie was a little quieter for the second half of the walk. Maybe I told a story about Roger and didn't notice.

The Eldest Skunk walked, and the walking was different from the walking she had done before. There was no destination. Rain fell, and the earthworms came to the surface. The earth here had less nitrogen, or calcium, or iron. It was sandier, or it had more clay; it wanted to be a hill when it grew up instead of the bottom of a bog. The worms tasted different from the worms the skunk had eaten before, because they came from a new place. The meat was rustier, and the slime was more like a squash blossom. She noticed the difference the way a person notices a stoplight turning from red to green. She was a skunk. She ate to eat, not to pay attention to her eating. The worms slid and stretched apart between her teeth and her pulse beat slower in gratitude.

She slept under a patch of ferns, the leaves arching over her like miniature forsythias. In the morning the sun came out. Her bones forgot their tiredness and remembered their elation. She was in a forest! The squirrels were louder here, away from the people, and the loam beneath her paws felt springy with decomposed moss. The moss had moved on, but it had left the ghosts of its rhizomes to pillow the soil. She moved like a little soap bubble, clean and new.

A skunk has a good sense of smell, and poor eyesight. This may be why skunks get run over by motor vehicles so often. They never see it coming. It's hard for people, with their good eyes and bad noses, to imagine a skunk's perspective. It would be better to stick with observable facts. The Eldest Skunk walked six miles from her forsythia. Skunks typically stay within one mile of their home, though males and adolescents sometimes go as far as five. The Eldest Skunk was living radically.

She ate earthworms until she was full, and then ate one more. Her stomach gurgled. She toiled with the shell of a fallen chestnut. Each spine stung the skin around her paws. There was beauty in the pain. The oriole had told her about flying for so long his wings felt like they might fall off, and then flying farther.

No. It's impossible to know if she was full, or if she was in pain.

Color, shape, patterns of movement. Things we can see.

Maybe it's deceitful to pretend we understand the skunks, but is there anything wrong with observing them?

A person on a porch, looking at a skunk in a lawn, seems permissible. The relationship isn't parasitic or symbiotic. It's the one in between, where one party benefits and the other doesn't notice.

But it's wrong to look at a teenage girl that way. There are words for that kind of looking: "ogle" and "leer." The creases in the flesh behind her knees, and the grape tendrils of hair at the nape of her neck—these are things that belong only to the girl. It could be dangerous for someone else to notice them. Not because the girl is delicate, but because it's terrifying to feel that the world is looking at you closer than you're looking at yourself.

Is a skunk different from a teenage girl? Is it okay to look?

*

The first encounter was the squirrels. The skunk was skirting the edge of a cold granite scent. Around her ankles lay whiffs of decomposing birch bark. Every few steps she kicked some of the smell up toward her nose.

Above her scuttered a pair of squirrels. Squirrels talk a lot. They called back and forth to each other about the colors of the leaves, and their hunger.

Green like a frog's forehead.

Green like a lime who is bracing itself for a career in vermilion to appease its mother.

Green like jumping from a pine tree to a maple.

Brown like satisfaction.

The squirrels have many more sounds for color than people do. For them, it doesn't take as many syllables to get the undertones across.

I'm hungry.

No, *I'm* hungry.

Well, I'm hungrier.

From down on the ground, the skunk could not tell the difference between green like a frog's forehead and green like jumping from a pine to a maple. She placed her forepaws on the trunk of the squirrels' current tree. In another moment the squirrels would be in a different tree. They wouldn't see her. But this first tree gave an infinitesimal sigh in response to her touch. It didn't go in for public displays of affection, but it lived for the moments when the wind nudged its uppermost twigs into the uppermost twigs of the tree next door. The squirrels felt the sigh. They looked down.

A skunk!

They skittered down four branches, and then up one.

Ahoy!

Hello, thought the Eldest Skunk. She thought about how she was looking for something without knowing what it was she was looking for. In a way, she was looking for something to look for. The squirrels wiggled down the main trunk of the tree, freezing when they were a few feet above the skunk. They pressed their bellies into the bark.

I'm always looking.

No, *I'm* always looking.

The squirrels looked at each other, and then switched places.

We're always looking.

We're looking for nuts.

There are two types of nuts, but we don't know which type we're looking for until we find them. There are new nuts we've never met before, and old nuts that we hid last year and forgot about.

Even when we find them, we don't always know. We might be mistaking old nuts for new ones. Or vice versa.

The Eldest Skunk pressed her belly into the leaf mulch, because she couldn't press it into the trunk of the tree. Thank you. She kept walking.

I FaceTimed my mother. She said I needed a haircut. I said how could she tell on such a small phone screen. My hair went past my shoulders. The way I had my camera angled, my face was bottom-heavy. My chin loomed, and she couldn't see most of the ends of my hair.

When was the last time you got a haircut? she asked.

I complained that she was my mother—shouldn't she be more concerned with my emotional well-being than with paltry aspects of my appearance? I made it sarcastic even though it was a real question.

A haircut *is* emotional well-being, she said. I'll pay for it.

After we hung up, I found Jan and Steve's kitchen shears and went to the bathroom. I pinched a piece of hair between my thumb and index finger. I moved my fingers up and down the hair. One inch? Two? Four?

Finally I let the scissors take a bite—an inch and a half from a single lock in front of my ear. Then I put the scissors back in their drawer. Lawn mower noises floated in the window from across the street. I got on my bike and pedaled to the hair salon.

At the front desk, I asked if they took walk-ins.

Yes, if I could wait twenty minutes.

They asked what I wanted. A trim, a blowout, a dye job?

I told them I would know in twenty minutes.

I flipped through the magazines. Some of them were about hair and some of them were about famous people. The skin of the hair models and the famous people didn't look like skin. It looked like pieces of computer-generated fruit. My mother was right. Haircuts helped people feel that who they had been yesterday didn't have to be who they would be tomorrow.

In the corner chair, a smock-draped client waited. There was a line of foil down the back of their head. What did the foil mean? Dye, a perm, deep conditioning? I made a deal with myself. I would have whatever the person in the corner was having. It wasn't a real deal because I had never been brave about hair decisions—I didn't expect myself to follow through.

I shut the magazine. I opened and closed a few apps on my phone.

When I looked up, the smock was being lifted; the chair was being turned. A middle-aged woman with masses of black hair stood up. There was a single white stripe down the center of her head. Her hair had the sort of volume mine had only dreamed of. It danced around her face. My breath stopped.

I pulled out my phone and typed *i think im hallucinating* into the box meant for drafting messages to Ellie. Then I deleted it. Our generation had cried wolf with words like "hallucinating" and "crazy." She wouldn't grasp the severity of the situation.

The hairdresser, who introduced herself as Shelley, was ready for me. She leaned my head back into the sink and asked if my neck was comfortable. I said yes. My neck hurt. The water and Shelley's hands were a lullaby. My follicles were a million little rocks in a million little brooks.

What are we thinking today? asked Shelley.

Just a trim, I said.

·

After the haircut I made sure not to look at myself in any store windows until I was around the corner from the salon. Then I stopped and studied my reflection in the glass over the menu for a Chinese restaurant. My hair looked flat. People talked about smoothness and shine as if they were desirable hair traits. When my hair was smooth and shiny, my face looked lonely in comparison.

Hey, said a voice from behind me. It was Eli. It was too much. Still—the downtown was small. To be in town was to be near the bakery. The run-in wasn't that unlikely. My subconscious might even have plotted it.

Hey, I replied.

Have you never been to this restaurant? he asked.

What?

Eli gestured at the storefront beside us. I mean, he said, you've been looking at the menu for a long time.

I blushed. Did the fact that he knew I'd been looking for a long time mean he'd been watching me for a long time? I admitted I hadn't been looking at the menu—I'd been looking at my new haircut.

Eli barked his bark-laugh. Once, in high school, I'd told him he seemed like a golden retriever person. Like, if he'd been a type of dog, he would have been a golden retriever. He'd been insulted. He'd said he was a cat person. He probably didn't remember this.

No shame, no shame, said Eli. Isn't it sort of the same length, though?

Was he admitting to having paid attention to how long my hair was, before? For a second I considered explaining: I'd attempted adventure, but the skunks had brought me back to myself. I needed a deep breath, not a quarter-life crisis.

It was just a trim, I said.

Eli nodded. Then he said he was glad he'd run into me. His house was having another little cookout thing on Friday. Did I want to come? It was very chill. I should bring a friend or two.

Oh! I said. Yes. I mean, thank you.

Sweet!

Then he was gone. He sort of bounced when he walked. Normally I didn't think of bouncy walks as attractive. He hadn't said what time on Friday, or where his house was. He was such a golden retriever.

I had a decision to make. It took me the whole bike ride home to decide: I would wait until Thursday—it was

Monday, now—to text him about what time the cook-out started. At home I lay on Jan and Steve's couch and scrolled back in my messages with Ellie. I tried to count how many times each of us initiated things. I often made this calculation in my messages with other people but had never done it in my messages to her. It turned out I initiated more of our text exchanges, and she initiated more of our in-person hangouts.

On Wednesday I texted Ellie about the cook-
out. Did she want to come?

She did.

On Thursday I texted Eli about the cookout. What time? What address? Should I bring anything?

Seven o'clock. 73 Bayberry Circle. Nah. There would be veggie burgers in case I was worried about that.

Ellie drove to my house, and I drove both of us from there. The need to conduct ourselves as a unit felt like high school, except that we hadn't gone to high school together. She wore a long flowered skirt with a sweatshirt from the local community college over it. The shapes weren't meant to go together. It made her look like a grown-up.

She angled her knees toward me from the passenger seat. She wanted to know what the game plan was.

I kept my eyes on the road. Eat veggie burgers? Pray they had s'mores?

Oh my God, said Ellie, oh my God. Can we stop at CVS on the way? I really need marshmallows now.

I mean, I said, they might already have them.

So then we'll have extra marshmallows.

We went to CVS. At the self-checkout, I asked Ellie if she knew that a baby skunk weighed the same as ten marshmallows. She stopped typing her PIN into the machine and turned to look at me. No, she said. Really?

The parking lot was starting to remember about sunset—that it existed, that it was on its way. The air was thinking about blushing gold. It was already 7:30. The rule was that you had to be late to parties if you didn't really know the people.

Take a picture of me with the marshmallows, said Ellie. She held them aloft like Simba in *The Lion King*. I took a photo.

So this is like, four baby skunks, she said.

She looked happy in the passenger seat. The skunks had been in my head so long, it was strange to hear someone else talk about them.

There were already three cars in Eli's driveway. A fourth car would have fit, but not without blocking the other three in. The house was yellow. It was one of those houses that's a ranch from the front, but sits on a hill so it becomes two stories in the back. I pulled onto the side of the road behind a telephone pole.

But seriously, said Ellie, where are you and Eli at these days? Does he know I know you guys hooked up? Are we allowed to joke about it?

No!

I tried to pull the key out of the ignition. It was stuck. I tugged and tugged.

We absolutely cannot joke about it, I said, still tugging at the key. I don't know him at all! I don't even know if he's dating anyone right now! Maybe his girlfriend is even here, at this cookout—or his boyfriend! Maybe he has a boyfriend!

Ellie frowned. She pointed at the gearshift. We were still in drive.

I shifted into park. The keys slid out.

Okay, said Ellie. Noted.

In the backyard there was a cinder block firepit, a charcoal grill, and a circle of people in camp chairs under a big tree. The circle was its own thing; it wasn't arranged around the firepit. There were more people than camp chairs, so some of the people were sitting on the grass.

Isabel! said Eli, turning. He was one of the people on the grass. He looked at Ellie. Wait, he said, fuck, I know your name. Strawberry Rhubarb Bar Girl.

Ellie beamed. Something twinged in my small intestine, like there was a cube of bread stuck there and someone was poking at it with a fondue fork. Eli was good at making people feel special. I already knew that. Seeing it in action still reminded me of my own un-specialness. It wasn't chemistry if he made everyone feel this way.

Ellie, said Ellie. Is my name. And your name is Eli, which is like, all the same letters, so you ought to remember.

Suddenly Eli and Ellie were having a debate about E's versus L's. Eli liked E's best. He thought that because Ellie's name also started with E, she would agree. Ellie felt more connected to L's. There were two L's in her name, right next to each other, as if they were good friends, and you had to say *L* out loud to pronounce them.

We joined the grass-sitters. Someone said we should do names and pronouns. We went around the circle and said names and pronouns. The only ones that stuck were Brynn (she/her) and Rachid (he/him), who didn't count because I'd already met them. Rachid looked less intimidating when he wasn't standing behind an espresso machine. I tried to decide if Brynn was actually a bitch, or if she still just had really good hair. She sat leaning back on her hands. Every so often she would move her knees from one side of her body to the other. In the Pilates classes I'd been listening to, this was called a "windshield wiper."

A boy whose name might have been Carl or Kyle told a story about a customer at a bike repair shop. The other half of the circle discussed local politics. There was drama on the school board. An election loomed. This half of the circle felt it was their duty to participate in local democracy. But they wondered if, having no school-aged children, they should abstain from the vote about who would chair the school board. In fact, they had sworn an environmentally motivated oath to never have children. What would an ideal system look like? Would parents' votes be weighted more than non-parents'? Would the non-parents' votes be further broken down into prospective parents and non-prospective parents?

Kyle or Carl had finished his bike repair story at this point. He cared about politics, too. He felt that categorization was the greatest evil facing mankind.

The greatest? said a girl in a camp chair. What about *global warming*?

Everyone laughed. The laugh didn't mean they were amused. The laugh meant they wanted a new subject of conversation.

A mosquito landed on my arm. I slapped at it. It flew away before my hand got to my arm.

Did you know, said Ellie, that a newborn skunk weighs the same as ten marshmallows?

She was still holding the bag of marshmallows. Her legs were crossed and the marshmallows were in her lap. Every so often she turned the bag over like she was fluffing a pillow.

Rachid whistled. Ten marshmallows?

Brynn windshield-wipered her knees to the other side. Now she faced Ellie more directly.

Kyle or Carl said he couldn't tell if ten was a lot or a little.

I should have seen it coming: Ellie ripping open the bag, Ellie handing the bag to Brynn, Brynn holding the bag while Ellie counted out ten marshmallows. She had to hug the already tallied marshmallows to her body with one hand while she counted with the other.

The marshmallows—the baby skunk—got passed around the circle. Ellie was on my left, and Eli was on my right. The marshmallows traveled clockwise. I would be last, and Eli second to last. Everyone's hands would touch them before mine did.

But a newborn skunk is smaller than this, right? asked Eli when it was his turn. He had both hands cupped in front of him. Everyone nodded. Eli thought this wasn't a good model, then. He pushed his hands together, compressing the marshmallows down to a more scientifically accurate size. They kept springing back.

There's only one option, said Eli.

Hold these, Isabel, said Eli.

He dumped nine marshmallows into my lap, grazing my thigh with the side of his palm. They bounced all over. There were marshmallows in the grass. There were marshmallows next to the crotch of my shorts. The tenth marshmallow, which Eli had kept, went into his mouth. He chewed. He didn't swallow. He spat it back into his hand. And it worked—the marshmallow was smaller and denser than before. His hands would have room for nine more.

Next, he said, opening his mouth wide and turning to me.

I put another marshmallow in and he chewed. He spat. He opened wide.

I couldn't look away from him. It was performance art. Eli chewed and spat. My arm moved from the grass to his lips. In his hand, the pile of slimy, white, sugary gelatin grew.

By marshmallow four, our audience began to shrink. Someone referenced the *Calvin and Hobbes* panel where Calvin stuffs his whole lunch into his milk carton. Brynn and Ellie started listing their favorite *Calvin and Hobbes* moments. I understood. Sometimes during makeover montages in movies, I stopped watching and scrolled around my phone. Once you understood what trope was being played out, there was no reason to look up until it was over.

Like, *everyone* touched these, didn't they? said Eli, between marshmallows, wiping his mouth on one wrist. He said it mildly, like he'd just realized he'd forgotten his umbrella, but it was okay because it probably wouldn't rain.

I said some of the marshmallows probably had my leg sweat on them.

No one mentioned that Calvin stuffs his lunch into his milk carton because of Susie. He wants to gross her out—he has a crush on her. No one wanted to talk about how *Calvin and Hobbes* upheld the patriarchy.

The spat-out marshmallows had teeth marks in them. I thought about dentists making retainer molds. I thought about how, in the black-and-white panels, Hobbes is a black-and-white-striped mammal. If there was meaning to this skunk parallel, instead of just coincidence, I didn't have time to decode it.

Last one, I said to Eli. It was the last marshmallow.

He chewed and spat. He looked at the glob in his hand. It was still larger than a newborn baby skunk. He squeezed the glob. A drop of saliva fell to the grass.

I expected him to ask if I wanted to hold it. The question would be joking and daring. If I said no, I would seem vanilla. If I said yes, I would seem desperate.

He didn't ask. He unfolded his legs and bounded over to the trash cans by the side of the house. Without any eulogy for our baby skunk, he threw the marshmallows in.

Coming back to the circle, he said he would never be able to eat a marshmallow again, ever in his life. He needed to, like, take a shot of mustard to get the taste out of his mouth.

I tried to decide if he'd sat down closer or farther away from me than before. Maybe farther away. Was it on purpose?

Try water? I suggested.

I took my water bottle from my bag and offered it. He took a swig. As in the moment in Jan and Steve's kitchen, earlier that summer, we couldn't be remembering the same thing. There was nothing very memorable about a post-hookup glass of water. I only remembered it because it had been my first.

Six years ago—in bed, in the sewing room, on top of the covers—Eli had said, "Do you want a glass of water?" He'd said it to break the silence. Before we'd kissed, I'd been the one less comfortable with silence, but after it was over, the roles reversed. I'd felt the sort of freedom that came with the last bell of the school day: my job was done and I could do as I pleased.

The Glass of Water had surprised me, as a step in the process. How many more such glasses would I drink in a lifetime? It had the intimacy of any ritual. It both moved you beyond the act, by washing away the flavor, and extended it by reminding you there was something to wash away. After I drank, I wished I'd waited. The flavor had been a new flavor, and now it was gone. I hadn't had time to come up with words for it. To understand what had happened, I would need to try again.

The water had been in a plastic souvenir cup from *The Lion King* musical on Broadway. I'd been grateful for this detail. It made everything easier—funnier, more irreverent—to explain to Claudia later.

Eli turned to ask Rachid if they should start grilling. I put my water bottle back in my bag. It was all coming back to me, now. There had been a book on Eli's nightstand, a title I'd heard of but hadn't read. I'd seen it before he kissed me, but only in the after-freedom had I been able to ask about it: Was it his? Did he like it?

He'd said it was good, so far. Had I read it? No? I ought to. Then we could talk about it.

On the drive home, I'd stopped at the library and gotten the book. I liked books, and I'd liked the idea of knowing what I was supposed to talk to Eli about. But in chorus on Monday, he hadn't sent any Snapchats. Or in chorus on Monday, I hadn't sent him any Snapchats. Either way it had been impossible to read the book. I'd returned it to the library unopened. Reading it would have been admitting I liked him more than he liked me.

At the cookout, we ate veggie dogs and drank blueberry hard ciders. The drink choices were blueberry hard cider or beer. I didn't like beer. When my second cider was halfway gone and I was sitting alone in a camp chair, peeling at the bottle's label, it occurred to me that I didn't like the cider either. It was sickly sweet. Why had

I picked it twice? Was it truly the lesser of two evils, or did it have to do with sexism? Had sexism made me keep choosing the sweeter drink, or made me regret adhering to something "girly," or both? The questions got tangled inside my brain. I let them go.

Ellie asked me to go to the bathroom with her. In the bathroom, she wondered out loud why there wasn't any bath mat. I said maybe they had put it away for the party because they didn't want people tracking mud on it. Ellie said I was always making excuses for boys. It hadn't rained in days. This was hardly a party.

I got mad at her for the next thing she said, but maybe it was really the making-excuses-for-boys comment that I was mad about.

The next thing she said was that Brynn was really hot, and could I ask Eli if she was single, slash, maybe get her number?

I frowned at myself in the mirror. Normally Ellie didn't include me in her romantic life. Normally she would mention at the end of a phone call that some girl had crocheted a shirt for her, and then a few months later she would text me a picture of the shirt with the caption *would u wear this?* because she and the girl had broken up. Maybe that sounds like involvement, but it wasn't. I never got to give advice.

Can't you ask her for her number yourself?

Part of Ellie's magic was her up-frontness. It didn't make sense for her to use interlopers.

Well, obviously, she said, pulling up her underwear. I was just giving you an opportunity to flirt with Eli by being joint wingmen. Jeez.

She hip-bumped me away from the sink so she could wash her hands. I stumbled into the shower curtain. We hadn't been drunk together before. Drunkenness was something that happened with school friends, and she'd always been my other friend. My school friends had measured how well they knew me by comparing how well they felt they knew *her*—the girl they met only through my stories. None of them would have recognized this Ellie. The Ellie they knew wasn't shiny or spiky. She didn't pursue hotness.

Ellie wiped her hands on her skirt. How many ciders had I had, she wanted to know.

Two.

She pursed her lips. Drink some water. You're driving.

Even Ellie was disappointed in me for being a lightweight.

We left the bathroom arm in arm. Either we had wordlessly made up, or we were adhering to the feminine pact about keeping whatever is said in bathrooms mysterious.

I wanted a graham cracker. I didn't want a s'more, only a plain graham cracker. No one else had thought about s'mores. By the fire, there was only our bag of marshmallows, with ten fewer marshmallows than it had started with. There was no chocolate. There were no graham crackers.

Inside, Eli was rinsing out red Solo cups in the kitchen sink.

We reuse them, he said. The environment. You know.

You don't have any graham crackers, I said. Do you?

He shook his head. Wheat Thins?

I thought about Wheat Thins. They weren't graham crackers, but they were surprisingly similar on an emotional level. I nodded. I said Eli owed me ten Wheat Thins, because of the ten marshmallows he'd chewed.

Okay, he said, but I can't feed them to you. My hands are wet. They're in the cabinet left of the fridge. No, the lower one.

Was it flirtatious that he'd brought up the possibility of feeding me, or was it unflirtatious because he'd said he couldn't? I left the kitchen once I'd counted out ten Wheat Thins. I didn't want to seem like I had any motivations beyond food.

Outside, Rachid had produced a guitar. The circle had reformed, this time around the fire. I asked Ellie if she wanted to leave. She nodded. We both felt that things were becoming too picturesque. Nothing unexpected could happen once a guitar came out. She picked up the leftover marshmallows and we walked away. In the safety of my car, she asked if I'd gotten what I wanted from the night. I couldn't answer. The streetlamps passed us off down the road like a fire brigade. Where one circle of light left off, the next began. I could never tell what I wanted. Ellie rolled down her window and the night air shuddered in, hot and muggy. What did I want? If I thought about it enough, the answer always seemed like "A Husband." As an answer, "A Husband" had no sense or dignity—I had no interest in sharing a bed or a mortgage with anyone—but if you said it with the right tone of voice you could make people laugh. Ellie wouldn't have laughed. This was both her blessing and her curse.

At home, in bed, I texted Eli. I was cultivating a feeling—the feeling of being on your phone when your parents thought you were asleep. Setting was everything in theater.

I sent the message in three pieces:

hey thank you thank you for the invite! it was v fun!

and

sorry we didn't say goodbye. ellie was being impatient

and

also Ellie wants Brynn's number lol

The detail about Ellie being impatient was a lie. That was what friends were for. They didn't mind being moved around for the sake of the plot.

I put my phone on vibrate under my pillow. Twice I found myself drifting off, and then pulled out the phone to see if I'd missed anything. I hadn't.

Eli sent me Brynn's number, and I forwarded it to Ellie. Four hours later, Ellie replied *lol I already have that.* Then our messages went like this:

! and?

and what

have u guys been talking

yeah

and??

wdym?

I stopped replying. I lay on the kitchen tile with my notebook. *Dear Ellie,* I wrote. *Did you want me to ask more about Brynn, or not? By not asking, am I being self-centered, or am I giving you privacy? Jeez. Sometimes I want to be a better person. Sometimes I want to slap you across the face.*

Evening light fell in stripes across the grouting. These were the sorts of things I could say to the Ellie in the notebook. I'd swept earlier in the day. Sweeping hadn't made me feel like an adult. It only reminded me of Cinderella. Real adults used vacuum cleaners.

Everyone seems to have a problem with the past or the future, I wrote. *I mean everyone is always looking for ways to feel new—haircuts and chest-opening yoga poses and fresh coats of paint. Does thinking about Eli mean I'm stuck in the past? Or am I thinking of him because of the emptiness of the future? Why am I supposed to get over him? What about reducing and reusing and recycling? Shouldn't we try to make something worthwhile from the things that are already in front of us?*

Sweat collected in the channel of my spine. If the mind was a sponge, then higher humidity decreased its capacity for further absorption. I couldn't tell if the metaphor made any sense. My shirt was scrunched up between the tile and my belly. The house had air conditioning, but Steve taught environmental science. Obviously use the air conditioning if you need to, Jan had said, but try to be sparing.

I rolled onto my back. Why was I here? The question tugged at my heart like the sleeves of an impractical blouse. I was so frivolous. Each evening, I opened all the windows. In the mornings I closed them, tugging the blinds to cover every possible inch of solar gain. This was to keep the house cool without technology. I was battling the climate crisis. I had so much time.

Ellie wanted to have a picnic. She said she would assign me what to bring. I was supposed to bring hummus and vegetables.

Only carrots? she said, peering into my bag.

We were in the woods, at the rock where I always went with Cecelia. Since Ellie had picked the menu, I got to pick the location.

You said hummus, I explained. That means carrots.

Carrots were my favorite vegetable to buy. They were the least expensive. They were what I already had in my fridge.

I said vegetables! That means cucumbers! Bell peppers! Celery, if you must!

Ellie was irate.

Ellie had brought goat cheese and fig chutney and a loaf of bread that echoed when you knocked on it. We straddled the rock and arranged the food between us. The bread was like taking a bite from a living coral reef, decadent and spongy.

Ellie said she hadn't brought a knife on purpose—tearing tasted so much better. She said it with her mouth full. It was one of those statements that everyone our age made, but made me think *this is why we're friends* when it happened to be *my* friend saying it.

Ellie asked if I knew what I was doing in the fall.

It had been a while since I'd been asked the question. I'd kept my shoulders turned away from it. That was the purpose of boys: they gave you something else to think about.

I said it looked like I was stuck here. This had been true since I took the yoga studio job. They needed someone through November, and I only had Jan and Steve's through August. I would need to find other housing, and most leases were yearlong, and at some point, things stopped being what you were doing "for now" and became what you were doing.

A glob of hummus fell from Ellie's carrot onto the rock. She swiped it up with her finger and put it in her mouth.

Interesting, she said, okay.

She dipped the empty carrot back into the hummus. This time it made it to her mouth all in one piece.

But, she said, couldn't you just stay at your dad's for two months? If you really wanted to leave? I mean, even the job. It's just a yoga studio. They could get someone else. If there was something else you wanted to do instead?

I shrugged. If. If there was something else.

Ellie wrinkled her nose at me. You goose, she said.

The sun lowered itself slowly onto its sofa at the end of a long day. Ellie was facing east, so the wisps of hair around her face went all Renaissance filigree. I was facing west, so my wrists, spreading goat cheese on a hunk of bread with a jammy spoon, looked smooth and tanned.

We talked about other things, and then, after we closed the hummus, Ellie asked about my love life.

I said I was trying not to think about boys as much. A big part of New Year's resolutions, I had read, was not getting discouraged by relapses.

Ellie laughed. What do you think about instead?

I almost said "skunks," but then Ellie suggested "girls?" and it was my turn to laugh.

She frowned. No, it's a serious question. Would you date girls, do you think?

I crossed my legs. Yes, no, maybe. I'd considered it. But it hadn't happened—there hadn't been any concrete possibilities.

Ellie frowned deeper. That seems untrue, she said. That seems more like you failing to recognize concrete things as possible.

Maybe my silence made Ellie feel bad, because then she said it didn't matter. All she meant was that girls could be nice. They planned cute dates. They gave you things. I could be getting fresh crusty bread for free, too! I needed to put myself out there.

What?

She waved what was left of the loaf of bread in the air. It was from Brynn, obviously! Or had Ellie not told me that Brynn worked at the bakery with Eli? She was forgetting how much I knew.

Maybe I didn't put enough goat cheese on my next bite, or maybe the bread tasted worse after that.

It's always a choice—what to count, and what not to count. The skunk walked onward. The wind exhaled, and a single maple seed that had withstood the winter's gales and the spring's blizzards fell down. She kept walking.

I biked to the library and checked out a copy of the book that had been on Eli's nightstand six years ago. The cover looked different from how I remembered Eli's looking. It showed a floating top hat. I couldn't remember what Eli's had shown, only that it hadn't been a floating top hat.

Standing in the silence between two bookshelves, I flipped through the book. The spine was in that rare flaccid condition of being equally happy to flop open to any page. No past reader had made more of an impression than any other. The book wasn't always trying to return you to page 179.

On my way out of the library, I paused by the stairs. This was the library I'd grown up with, not the one in Jan and Steve's town. There was a small art gallery on the top floor. My father never went to this library without visiting it. He used to lift me up so I could stare at the paintings straight on. Remember, he would say, no art is above you.

I took the stairs two at a time. Today the gallery was filled with pen-and-ink sketches. The one to the left of the door showed a laundry line with a disproportionate number of bras. Then again, maybe the garments on the line were only the ones that couldn't be tumble dried.

I backed up and skimmed the ABOUT THE ARTIST brochure on the stool by the door. The gallery only ever showed local artists, which meant artists that had day jobs. This one was a bank teller. Maybe bank tellers wore bras more often than yoga studio receptionists. Still—no one I knew washed their bras with any frequency. Maybe the drawing showed a special occasion. The bank teller wanted to signal a new beginning. She would wash all her bras at once and start anew.

I planned to walk quickly around the room. Lingering in front of artwork was almost always performative. At the second to last drawing, I stopped. This one was larger than the others. At first it seemed to be a Noah's ark variation. Animals flooded a living room. Two owls roosted on the top edge of a flat-screen TV. Bats hung from the ceiling fan. A bear in an easy chair opened a picture book so that everyone could see. The piece was titled *Story Time*. Coming down the stairs at the side of the room was a single skunk.

The universe shook its head at me in disapproval. I left the library without looking at the final drawing.

At the grocery store, there was a sale on grapes. The sign had a big yellow number printed on it. I thought it was the price per bag. At the register, watching the numbers come up on the screen behind the cashier, I realized it was the price per pound.

Actually, I said, no grapes. I've changed my mind. I'm sorry, is that totally annoying?

The cashier assured me it wasn't annoying. She put the bag of grapes on a small counter behind her, canceled the transaction, and started again on the items she'd already packed into my shopping bag. Milk, eggs, carrots.

The buttons on the PIN pad blurred. There had been no reason not to buy the grapes. Eli hadn't contacted me since the cookout. I was used to feeling like the things I wanted were bad for me. I blinked furiously.

It was a good book. It grabbed me. I carried it places—except "places" only ever meant "the yoga studio"—under my arm.

The book was about a man who had relations with women. Some of the women were his friends. One of the women was his wife. He was in love with the wife. The relations were all sexual. His wife was sincere and distressed by infidelity. She was the sort of woman you were supposed to avoid becoming. The friend-women were more likeable, though they didn't get the guy. I wondered if those were my two options: single and happy, or partnered and distressed. But no—that couldn't be true. What the women *wanted* mattered more than what they *had*. I could desire a relationship and be unhappy, or not desire a relationship and be content.

While the Pilates students rolled up their mats, I placed the book face down on the desk, open to the page where I'd left off.

Stacy came out of the studio last. She set her water bottle next to the book. She rooted through her bag for a comb, squinting at the cover. A comb, a bottle of dry shampoo, a hair tie, and a compact mirror migrated from her bag to the desk.

Isn't that book supposed to be sort of misogynistic? she said, spraying a cloud of dry shampoo onto her hairline.

What?

Stacy shrugged. She thought she recognized it from one of those fuckboy starter pack memes. But she was old. She didn't understand the internet.

Oh, I said. Maybe. I'm not sure.

She combed her hair into a fresh ponytail with tiny strokes, then picked up the compact mirror to inspect her work. Next came lip balm, which had been hiding in a secret pocket of her leggings. She said she used to read books. She said I should try to avoid growing up. Now that her lips were moisturized, she could leave. She hoped I would have a good weekend.

I wheeled my swivel chair out from behind the desk and over to the box fan. All the students were gone. Stacy was gone. It was time to go home. Had the lip balm been the last step in her post-workout beauty routine, or was she even now swiping mascara on in the front seat of her car? I picked up the book and kept reading.

Another difference between the friend-women and the wife-woman was that the wife was a virgin before she met the man. The wife stood naked in front of him and he felt responsible. He felt excited to guide and protect.

I hadn't lost my virginity to Eli. He'd only guided and protected.

I wondered if how the man in the book saw the world was also how High School Eli saw the world. In high school, maybe I'd seemed like a wife-type. That was why he'd had to turn away. He hadn't been ready for that kind of responsibility. Now I was getting invited to barbecues. What did it mean? Was it possible to cross over? Could I have become a friend-type? Or was he ready to settle down?

I understood my problem. Then and now, I was a wife-type trying to pass myself off as a friend-type. It was a problem because I never knew if I'd succeeded. Maybe Eli hadn't considered his actions a "turning away." If we'd only ever been friends, nothing had begun or ended.

I put away the box fans and went home. Before, I would have described the book as "honest," but maybe Stacy was right. Maybe the word I was looking for was "misogynistic." I was eating it up.

The second obstacle was a mushroom and a violently blue butterfly. They existed as a unit. It wouldn't make sense to think of them as separate obstacles.

The mushroom was shaped like a folded parasol, tall and narrow. It wore the butterfly like a hat, and the butterfly wore the mushroom like a plinth. Neither moved a muscle. Even if it had been part of a stop-motion movie of fungi blossoming, the mushroom would have sat still for as long as the butterfly cared to stay.

The skunk looked only for a moment. She couldn't go over it, and she couldn't go under it. She backed up. Once she was far enough away that she wouldn't have been able to feel the breeze created by a flap of the butterfly's wings, she turned north and moved forward again. She walked a wide arc around the spot where she knew the woods were already full.

Cecelia's family returned from Maine. Jon opened the door with his headphones around his neck and his glasses perched in his hair. He looked older and younger—tired and inspired. It was great, he said.

They'd gone on a whale watch and Cecelia had been all confused about why the whales didn't look like her whale stuffed animal. We should have warned her they weren't going to be orcas, he said. Anyway, she's in the TV room.

Jon and Amelie kept the TV in the guest bedroom, away from the living area. Cecelia lay on the bed on her stomach. She was watching a program about anthropomorphized trains.

Okay, I announced to the room, Isabel's here, no more TV.

I always felt like a substitute teacher when I talked about myself in the third person.

Cecelia shook her head. Her eyes didn't move from the screen. The episode isn't over, she said.

I put my hands on my hips. Then I put them back at my sides. For a second, I tried to tune in to what was happening in the show. The trains were singing. One of the trains needed a part replaced, and the other trains were going to work together to help it. From previous arguments with Cecelia, I knew that every episode followed the same format. Right now, the trains were racing along the track to find their missing friend. That meant it was less than half over.

Okay, I said, but you can finish it later. Haven't you seen this one before?

She didn't respond.

That's the rule, I said. No TV when the babysitter is here. I'm sorry.

She kept looking at the TV.

I'm going to turn off the television now, Cecelia.

I clicked the power button on the base of the TV set. Cecelia screamed and planted her face in the blankets.

I sat down beside her.

Do you want to read a book? Or go to the stream?

You're mean, Cecelia said into the mattress.

I sighed and picked up a picture book from the bedside table. In general, I believed in no mercy. There was psychology behind it: something about kids needing structure and strict boundaries in order to feel safe. The picture book had a lobster boat on the cover.

Is this new? I asked. Did you get it in Maine?

Cecelia scooted away from me.

I read the book out loud. Even though the main characters were the fishermen, all the lobsters had smiley faces. I found this disturbing. Weren't we supposed to *like* the fishermen? Why were the illustrators emphasizing the subjectivity of the protagonists' victims? Was it meant to prepare children for the real world?

Cecelia turned onto her back and stared at the ceiling, heaving great sighs every minute or so. The book ended. I put it back on the side table and resisted the urge to take out my phone.

Okay, I said, we're going to the park.

I left her in the TV room while I packed the snack bag. In this instance, I believed in the healing power of a change of scenery. At the park, Jon would be out of earshot. There would be no audience for my weak attempts at discipline.

But Cecelia followed the rules. She Velcroed her shoes by herself. She took my hand when we got to the crosswalk. Her palm, in my fingers, stayed limp.

I asked about the vacation. Had it been fun?

Yes.

Had she gone swimming?

Yes.

What was her favorite part?

Ice cream.

What flavor of ice cream did she get?

Lobster Tracks.

What was in Lobster Tracks?

She didn't remember.

Normally, when Cecelia and I hadn't seen each other for a while, she would turn up taller and tanner and more talkative than she'd been before. A few weeks mattered. Time was moving forward, taking her with it. Like always, I could see that she was older. This time, though, the differences weren't physical. This time she had learned to hold a grudge.

She climbed up the slide, ignoring the ladder, and slid back down. She did it again. And again. The slide was in a spiral shape. Each time she climbed up, she placed her feet in exactly the same spots along the plastic curve. I sat down on the center of the seesaw. Déjà vu and vertigo were cousins.

The hours passed. When it was time for me to leave, Cecelia watched Jon count out the cash from his wallet and hand it to me.

Can I watch TV now? she asked him.

Jon rubbed the bridge of his nose.

I shut the door behind me. It was the time of year when you could see just by looking who watered their lawns. Jon and Amelie's grass was brown. Across the street, little red flags with danger symbols marched around a crisp block of green. I wished I'd biked instead of driven. I never biked to Cecelia's. There were too many hills; it was too far. As I drove, the car radio told me about the stock market. I didn't register if the stock market was going up or down, only that the reporters were using their stock market voices. When I turned off the ignition at Jan and Steve's, I realized I'd forgotten to buy milk. That morning, I'd used the last of it, thinking I would stop and get more on the way back from Cecelia's. I put my forehead on the steering wheel and sobbed.

That same night, Jon and Amelie sent a text asking if I could babysit on Friday evening. The independent cinema was having a Fellini retrospective. Their first date, back in college, had been to see a Fellini movie. Today the film was online. Anyone could rent it and watch it on their couch, but Jon and Amelie wanted to experience the magic of a large dark room. And to support local businesses, if I was free.

Really though, they said in a separate text message, only if you're free. It's a Friday! You're young!

I tapped on the oval where you were supposed to type replies. I hovered my fingers above the keyboard, then set the phone down.

On my computer, I navigated to the cinema's website. Tickets were twelve dollars. I watched the trailer. A man spoke in Italian. White letters superimposed across the bottom of the screen spoke about wanting to create a perfect film. For the white letters, perfection meant truth. I didn't like the man. It was so typical of him to equate truth and beauty. It also explained why all the women around him wore dark eyeliner. He was clearly the type to fall for it—to think that was really what their eyes looked like.

I put a single ticket in the virtual cart, then closed the window without paying. Jon and Amelie might have other babysitters up their sleeves. Or they might not, and then I would be alone in a movie theater with no intrigue.

I told Jon and Amelie I couldn't do it.

It had been kind of them to think I might be busy. I didn't need to shatter the illusion. Besides—telling Cecelia to stop watching TV frightened me. It frightened me both when she didn't listen and when she did.

On Friday evening I picked up my phone. It was 6:47 PM. It was only four minutes later than the last time I'd picked up my phone. I lay on the carpet with my ankles underneath my knees and peeled my spine off the floor one vertebra at a time. I am young, I said out loud. I am young.

At 7:23, I had a sudden desire to go Night Swimming. Night Swimming was something people always pronounced as if it had capital letters, as if it were separate from normal swimming. At first, my desire embarrassed me. Probably I didn't want to swim at all. Probably I only wanted to feel bleak and romantic. I got on my bike.

The roads to the pond were empty. The sky was gray-orange, like Cecelia's playdough after she made "pizza," not realizing the colors couldn't be unstuck. I tried to keep the wheels of the bike in between the two yellow lines. It worked better when I was looking ahead instead of at the lines—but of course this was hard to verify. If I was looking ahead, how could I be sure of where the wheels were?

It wasn't a good pond. To get in you had to wade through a ring of mud. I sat on the log where people always left their clothes and waited for it to get dark. At least I didn't see any high schoolers. That had been another reason not to come. The pond was—or used to be—a popular party spot. I'd never gone to the parties, only seen the videos on social media the morning after.

In high school, I'd assumed teenage boys got less scary once you were older than they were. But the reverse had happened. Now they could wield their youth over me, too.

The clouds reflected in the water turned from flat and orange to shiny and deep. I took off my clothes. I'd been coming here since I was small. Ellie's and my parents used to stay on the shore while we swam. We'd debate which inch of skin was most sensitive to the first lick of cold water: the backs of our knees, the upper inner thigh, the belly button? Then we'd dive in and practice wiggling our spines like the mermaids on that show about Australian mermaids.

I dove in. That was something that deserved capital letters: Swimming Where You Got the Top of Your Head Wet versus swimming where you didn't. There were other words for it: Total immersion. Baptism.

In one morning-after video, Eli and Damien had stood waist-deep in the water, howling at the moon.

Tonight, the moon looked down at me like a nanny from another era. It had lots of children to look after, and I could become an astronaut if I had anything important to say. I tried to howl, still doggy paddling. It came out shivery and thin. This had less to do with the doggy paddling and more to do with being a girl. I couldn't convince myself to let go and make noise. Then I got embarrassed about not being able to make noise. Then I realized the anticipation of the embarrassment was one of the things holding me back in the first place. Most things worked in circles.

Back on shore, I jumped up and down to shake off the water before putting my clothes on. The bushes rustled. I froze.

No one appeared. I put my shirt on, keeping my elbows close to my body. My hair dripped metronomically down my back. The bushes rustled again, farther away. The rustle was larger than a squirrel but smaller than a human. I let my elbows get farther from my body. Why had I assumed the noise came from a human? There were other active beings exerting their wills on the world. There were possums and raccoons. On the walk back to my bike I turned my phone flashlight on, examining the plants by the trail. Poison ivy; Virginia creeper; winterberry. There was no skunk cabbage in sight, but the smell was in the air. Could it have originated with the animal rather than the plant? It seemed like too much to hope for. I'd read articles about trees communicating through their root systems. Did skunks have root systems, too? Could a skunk in a yard and a skunk near a pond agree that they had seen the same girl?

I couldn't avoid Cecelia forever. Jon and Amelie asked if I could help her sort her stuffed animals. She was getting a new bed. The big-girl bed took up more space and didn't have a railing. To make room for maturity, she had agreed to cull some of her belongings.

Jon gave us two big boxes, one labeled KEEP and one labeled TOSS. Cecelia couldn't read, but she knew which was which. She knew *K* and *T*.

I picked up a stuffed llama. What about this guy? I asked.

She snatched it out of my hands.

I can do it myself, said Cecelia. I have a *system*. And Llamalina is a girl.

Llamalina went into the KEEP box. So did a pig and a Winnie-the-Pooh. A unicorn and Caroline, the orca whale, went into TOSS. Cecelia worked quickly, never hesitating once she'd picked someone up. I felt almost insulted on Caroline's behalf. It was one thing to be tossed, and another to be tossed with no regrets. Two years earlier, Cecelia hadn't been able to fall asleep without her.

I fingered the whale's flipper where it hung over the edge of the cardboard. The plush had been worn down into solid nubbins. Are you sure about Caroline? I asked.

Cecelia nodded. Yes, she said. It's my *system.*

A dragon with reflective wings went into TOSS.

When all the animals were sorted, I asked what the system had been. How had she known where to put everyone?

I kept all the real animals, she said. Duh.

Cecelia stood up and moved two of the KEEP animals—the pig and an owl—back to their spot on her bedside table.

What do you mean? I asked.

All the animals that really exist, Cecelia repeated.

I stared at the boxes.

What about Winnie-the-Pooh? I asked.

He's a bear, she said. Bears are real.

But Cecelia, I said, whales are real, too. Caroline is a whale.

No, she said, she's an orca.

And orcas are a type of whale. They're real.

Cecelia put her hands on her hips. Isabel, she said, you don't have to pretend. I'm a big girl now. I know orcas are fake, like Santa.

I made her sit down on the small-girl bed with me.

Who told you orcas are fake?

She hugged her knees to her chest. Daddy and Mommy. On the whale watch. We only saw other kinds of whales, and I asked why, and Daddy said because the orcas live far away, like at the North Pole and stuff. And the North

Pole isn't real. That's where Santa and the elves and the pretend things are.

She'd tilted her chin down so she was looking up at me even though we were pretty much level.

I crossed my legs so the other one was on top. I opened my mouth, and then shut it. It seemed like a moment when I could justify exposing her to technology. We started with a map of the world, huddling together over my phone. The area at the top, I explained, was the North Pole. It was a real place, but the reality of the thing was different from the way people sometimes imagined it to be. There was a lot of ice and cold water, but no elves or toy workshops. And in the ice and water, there were sometimes orca whales.

I pulled up photos of the whales, as well, but somehow those were less convincing. Something about the crisp black-and-white lines over the aquarium-blue water looked computer-generated.

I took Caroline out of the TOSS box and handed her to Cecelia. She wiggled the dorsal fin back and forth without looking at me.

We can go ask your dad, if you want, I said. He'll explain. I think you just misunderstood. But it makes sense why you thought that. I liked your logic.

She shrugged.

I stood up and pushed the boxes to a strip of bare wall by the door. A pair of footie pajamas lay crumpled on the dresser. I tried to straighten them out, but the footie parts wouldn't stay folded.

Isabel, Cecelia whispered, what about the skunks?

I turned to face her. She was holding Caroline tight to her stomach, her mouth all pinched and serious. My fingers tensed involuntarily on the pajamas. What do you mean?

Are they real?

She blinked at me, twice.

Yes, I said, skunks are real.

Cecelia threw Caroline to the floor and lay back on the bed, hands over her face.

I don't get it, she wailed. Why did Mommy and Daddy eat the mustard?

The night of Skunk Christmas, they'd set out the cards and the plate of mustard on the porch, just like they set out cookies and letters for Santa. Cecelia hadn't been able to sleep. She knew she wasn't supposed to peek, but she couldn't help it. She got out of bed and looked out the window. And there were her parents, eating the mustard that she'd left for the skunks!

I know they eat the cookies for Santa, she told me, because Santa doesn't exist, so he can't eat them himself. But if the skunks exist, then why would they eat the mustard? Why didn't they leave it for the skunks?

Oh Cecelia, I said.

She sat up and looked at me, eyebrows all scrunched together. I reached out one finger and ran it down her forehead.

Do you want me to braid your hair? I asked.

She frowned. A beat of silence. Can you do a French braid?

We got her *Little Mermaid* hairbrush from the bathroom. Ariel's face had almost worn off the plastic handle, but it was the only brush she'd accept. She sat on my lap, facing away.

I tried to explain that things didn't always act the way you wanted them to. We couldn't control other people, let alone skunks. Skunks probably didn't like mustard. Out of all the things her father had told her, that was the only lie.

She nodded slightly, the hair between my fingers going taut then slack. There were tangles at the nape of her neck, a collection of knots like little burrs. I would just braid them in. It wasn't a moment for pulling.

At the pond, the Eldest Skunk had her third and final epiphany. The pond came to her like the evening, gradually and then all at once. Suddenly she recognized the smells that had already been in her nostrils. There was mud, and skunk cabbage, and the dissolved egg jelly the tadpoles had left behind. A pond. Not knowing the name "skunk cabbage," she felt no affinity for the plant. She drank. The skunk in the water drank, too.

Mud nestled between the pads of her feet. She wanted to tell the oriole that the skunk in the water had followed her. Would the oriole call it failure or success, to find the familiar so far from home? Was it a comfort, or a rendering moot of her journey?

A line of ducks arced across the water. Mother and babies. Counting still wasn't instinctual for the skunk, so she didn't notice how many there were. The mother duck floated, while the ducklings attempted to float and became frustrated when it came out as paddling. Their tails gave them away, vibrating above the water. They couldn't hide how much hard work went into moving forward.

The mother dove straight downward. She did not say "Wait here, darlings." The ducklings knew to wait. They might have waited forever and not noticed. Their mother might have been eaten by a snapping turtle at the bottom of the pond, and the ducklings would have stayed. To a duckling, there is nothing embarrassing in waiting for something you love. The point of something you love is that it will come back.

The mother duck returned, and the ducklings broke formation. They paddled around her like ants celebrating a stale breadcrumb. The mother distributed pondweed.

The skunk rested her chin on her paws, but kept her haunches raised. The oriole used to distribute earthworms to his children like that. How many of his children were still alive?

The ducks fell back into line, and the skunk remembered to count.

One.

It wasn't the oriole that she wanted. The oriole was far away, and skunks do not wish for sunshine when it's raining.

Two, three, eleven.

It was time to go home. The Eldest Skunk ran as if there was a bear chasing her, even if it was a bear she'd left her house explicitly to find. Eleven, eleven, eleven!

I picked up my phone from the nightstand.
There was a text from an unknown number. The text had
been sent at 11:12 PM. From this, I knew the sender had
something I didn't: a reason to stay awake in the evening.

*hi Isabel. hope you're doing well. was wondering if you
would want to get coffee sometime? and gossip etc?*

I brushed my teeth and racked my brains. Yes, I'd imagined writing my name and number on countless receipts.
I'd picked out people on park benches that I might give
the receipts to: the one with the *Goodnight Moon* tote
bag, the one using a copy of *The Bell Jar* as a sun visor
while they watched their friends play tennis. I'd never
done it.

At 7:27 AM I replied.

Sorry, who is this?

I took a sip of instant coffee. It needed a half splash
more milk. I crossed to the fridge. By the time I was back
at the table, there was a new notification.

brynn lol
i thought Eli had given u my number
oh well!

So Brynn had reasons to be awake in the morning as well as in the evening. Maybe I'd already known that—she worked at a bakery. In what context had Eli told her I'd asked for her number? He'd sent me the number, but I hadn't saved it in my contacts. Brynn was for Ellie.

Oh! I typed. It was too late to pretend to be someone who didn't start sentences with capital letters.

Yes, sure, what day?

I hovered over the send button. Then I deleted *what day?* and replaced it with *maybe Saturday?* In Brynn's world, I could still be someone with a busy schedule.

Athena meowed.

You've already been fed, I told her.

She meowed again. I picked up her water dish and dumped it into the sink. The inside of the bowl felt slightly slimy. I ran my fingers around it under the faucet until it felt clean. What did that word mean—gossip? It meant something to do with Ellie, I decided. Brynn would want to know what her deal was, or if she was looking for a relationship. Ellie hated to be talked about.

•

On Saturday, there was a ring of condensation on the table left from the last customer. I ran my sleeve over it. I'd worn long sleeves in preparation for the air conditioning.

The Black Sheep had been Brynn's choice. By choosing it instead of the bakery, was she avoiding the politics of giving me free food, or avoiding being seen by Eli? When I questioned men's motives, the options were either a) the reason I thought they had done something or b) the reason I hoped they had done something. But Brynn wasn't a man. I honestly didn't know what she wanted. She was harder to predict, or I had fewer preferences about her feelings.

I got there first and claimed the booth seat. Across the room, a teenage girl lifted her phone to take a photo of her friend. Then she lowered the phone. She rearranged their coffee cups. The cups were tall and iced and green. The friend moved her own phone off the table and undid her ponytail. They tried again.

It was four minutes past the hour Brynn and I had agreed on. Picking up my phone to check the time felt like asking your parents "Are we there yet?" on a long car ride.

I hadn't told Ellie I was meeting Brynn. Without knowing Brynn's motives, what was there to tell? That was the excuse I rehearsed in my head. Maybe I was being selfish. I wanted to pretend the meeting was about me, not about Ellie.

At eight minutes past, Brynn pushed open the door. She didn't have a bag, or long sleeves. She stood behind the chair across from me and bit her lip.

Do you want to go someplace else? she asked.

What?

I don't know. Ice cream? She crossed her arms. Rachid isn't here, and I only picked here because I thought he might report back to Eli. And then it would be, I don't know. Drama. It's too late in the day for coffee.

Across the room, the phone girls scooted their chairs next to each other. They leaned in, inspecting the photos. With their heads right next to each other, you couldn't tell where one girl's hair started and the other's began. They were both blonde. Brynn and I left the café.

In the car, with her feet flat on the floor of the passenger side, Brynn was surprised I hadn't taken a Pilates class. She used to date a Pilates instructor.

You should try it, she said. It's good for you. Not the exercise, but the experience. Like going to a restaurant by yourself.

In line for ice cream, I asked what she'd meant about Rachid, and Eli, and causing drama.

Shh, she said. She kept her eyes on the list of flavors. Cookie dough or purple cow. Cookie dough or purple cow?

She said it twice, like the names might reveal something.

Hanging pots of mums decorated the eaves of the farm stand. We were still in line. Which one is your favorite? she asked.

I pointed to a pot of yellow mums at the end of the row.

Hmm, said Brynn. Yes, that one is very you.

We took our ice creams to the picnic tables behind the farm stand building. Brynn had grown up in Albuquerque. Her two little brothers still lived there with her mom. Sometimes she missed the pesto rolls from the city food co-op, and the little brothers. Her dad had come here first. He'd taken an administrative position at the university, which meant she could follow him here while pretending it was only because of the free tuition. Now he was off at Stanford. Brynn was twenty-four. She ate her ice cream slowly, with the tip of her tongue. She didn't know if she would move back to Albuquerque in one year or in ten.

When I finish my ice cream, she said, we'll talk for real.

I liked her talent for suspense.

And until then?

Tell me a story.

I was halfway done with my cone. She hadn't bitten into hers. There was still a smooth hemisphere of purple cream rising above it. There was still a tiny spot of gluey paper stuck to the bottom of mine. I took another bite.

Hmm, I said. Once upon a time there were three skunks.

A toddler at the next picnic table screamed. Their ice cream had fallen from the cone into the gravel.

William! said the adult who was with them. This is why I told you to get it in a bowl!

William sobbed harder.

Brynn and I watched in silence. The sun went behind a cloud and the hairs on my arms stood up straighter. I felt full of love for these people, who were putting their lives on display. We were all William—choosing wrongly, even when others warned us it would lead to despair. We were all adults—wringing our hands at youth.

And? said Brynn. What were their names?

Whose names?

The skunks.

Oh. Skunks are very private about their names, I said. They don't tell just anyone.

Brynn nodded. That makes sense.

I'm sorry, I said. I don't know what happens next.

I meant in the story she'd asked for, but maybe Brynn understood my words differently. She tucked the bottom half of her cone into her napkin, uneaten. I guess, she said, we need to talk about Eli.

I thought I'd misheard, or she'd misspoken.

About Ellie, you mean?

Brynn frowned. She turned toward me on the picnic bench so she was sitting crisscross applesauce.

No, she said. Eli. The tall one with curly hair. The guy we're both fucking?

I tore off a corner of a paper napkin and stuffed it into the space between the boards of the picnic table. Three Canada geese flew overhead, honking, though it wasn't the season for migration. The pieces of the world were up in the air, waiting to rearrange themselves before falling back to earth. Where would they land? What was happening?

I'm not fucking Eli, I said.

Oh.

Brynn got up and put her ice cream in the trash, then sat back down.

I guess I just assumed—

She closed her mouth again.

I shook my head. In high school, I said, once. But not now.

Welp, said Brynn. *Now* I look like a jealous not-even-girlfriend. God.

Brynn had met Eli when he started working at the bakery, when she was still dating the Pilates instructor. At first they were just coworkers. They had a running argument about if Brynn got more tips because she was a better barista or because she was a girl.

That's the thing about Eli, said Brynn. He *sucks*, but I like him anyway.

Then the Pilates instructor told Brynn she wanted an open relationship. Brynn agreed. Brynn and Eli had sex. A month later, the Pilates instructor changed her mind. She brought Brynn a bottle of wine and said let's be monogamous. Brynn said no, it doesn't work like that, you can't just go back and forth. Polyamory agreed with her. So Kendra—that was her name, the Pilates instructor—felt like Brynn was prioritizing Eli over her. Kendra and Brynn broke up.

Brynn still felt bad about it all. She'd told Kendra the breakup didn't have anything to do with Eli, but maybe it had. Maybe Kendra had been right.

I had a whole row of napkin pieces stuffed into the crack in the table at this point. A sunburn whispered at the back of my neck. I didn't want to make any sudden movements. *Keep talking, keep talking.* I prayed like I was praying for a stoplight to stay green.

Brynn didn't know why she was telling me this. It wasn't my problem.

But what's happening now? I asked. Why did you think Eli and I—?

Brynn looked me up and down.

I'm sorry, she said. I'm confused. Like, if you and Eli aren't hooking up, are you friends? Am I making weirdness for you two by telling you all this? Is what I say here going to get back to him? Would you admit it if it was?

I lifted my hands, helpless. How could I explain to Brynn that I felt loyal to her in a way I would never feel toward Eli? She was a girl who liked pesto and missed her father.

Eli and I don't really know each other, I said. We have, like, context without substance.

What does "substance" mean?

Any real knowledge of each other as people? Chemistry?

You have chemistry, said Brynn. Trust me.

At the start of June, Eli told Brynn that a girl he'd gone to high school with would be house-sitting for his parents. He said it when he and Brynn were lying naked in bed. He'd orgasmed, but she hadn't. He talked about the house-sitting in terms of his relationship with his parents, and belonging and approval. Then he asked if Brynn still wanted him to go down on her. Or was she all set?

She was all set.

The day after the cookout, when they were alone together in the bakery, he told her he'd hooked up with me in high school. Brynn was cleaning underneath the rack of to-go cup lids. Eli was behind the register, working on a crossword.

Did I ever tell you, he said, that Isabel and I hooked up in high school? Yeah. Anyway. Seven letters, tired. Any ideas?

It was the fact that he'd kept it a secret so long that made Brynn suspicious. She wanted to know more. She wanted to know why he'd suddenly decided she needed the information.

Oh, Brynn said, stacking the lids. She seemed cool.

Eli looked up. Sorry, what?

She seemed cool.

Who?

Isabel.

Oh! Yeah. Yeah, she is.

Eli went back to his crossword.

I didn't know how to say anything else without seeming suspicious, said Brynn. You know? But I was suspicious! Or frustrated, or unsatisfied, or something. He never tells me things. But I didn't know if my annoyance was justified. Sometimes there's nothing to tell. So finally I was like, okay, if I want to know more about Isabel, I should talk to Isabel.

A family that had ordered multiple banana splits arrived at the edge of the seating area. The children hadn't been allowed to carry their splits. Adult hands held the paper sundae trays aloft. The children trotted beneath like dogs at puppy kindergarten. Unlike William, they wouldn't make their own mistakes.

Brynn and I ceded our table.

Since we'd driven from town in one car, and since the sky was the blue of a free-range farmers market egg, we didn't say goodbye. We started discussing where to go next without asking the question. Brynn said I was the local guide.

Surprise me, she said. It's your turn, though.

So I told her my story.

He was a bass and I was an alto. I added Damien on Snapchat; Eli added me. There was a party at the pond, and a video of Eli and Damien howling at the moon.

After chorus that Monday, Eli caught up with me in the hallway. He'd never sought me out in public before. Damien's into you, he said. You should go for it.

So the next weekend I hooked up with Damien. It sounds oversimplified, and it felt that way in real life, too. There'd been so many years of kissing feeling like an impossibility that could only happen to other people. Then, suddenly, it was something that could happen very easily. It didn't make sense.

That's exactly how it was for me, too, said Brynn. Can I turn down the air conditioning?

I nodded. She reached for the dial.

Damien and I did things besides kiss, too, mostly because they offered a clear ending point. An orgasm was a way of knowing when the interaction was over without having to speak about it. While I put on my clothes, he told me about the pond conversation. Before or after the howling, Eli had apparently identified me as "pretty hot." Months later, I hooked up with Eli. But that hookup didn't matter as much. Eli had already changed my life.

Driving home from Damien's house in my father's car—I'd borrowed it claiming I was going to Claudia's—I felt like a little soap bubble. I didn't know anything more about sex than I had two hours before, but now I would be allowed to talk about it as if I did. I called Claudia on speakerphone. She cried. I'm proud of you, she said, I just expected to be first.

On Monday, I understood the full extent of the change. Danny Gonzales nodded to me as I was putting my coat in my locker. Danny Gonzales hadn't previously acknowledged my existence, though our lockers had been next to each other all year. Hey, Isabel, he said. Did you have a good weekend?

Brynn slapped her knee. That is *so* classic, she said. I mean, that is straight out of a movie.

At lunch, all *my* friends reported being asked by *their* friends to confirm or deny the event. Damien hadn't hooked up with anyone before, either, so it was big news.

I considered driving to the pond, but I wanted a place untainted by history. I picked the shoe store. It was next to the supermarket. You parked on the same ocean of pavement. Seagulls roosted on the lamp poles, and the sea was hours away.

Does this place have cheese samples? Brynn asked as we pulled in.

I don't think so, I said. But we're here to look at shoes, not food.

She laughed. I forget, she said, that girls are so much more creative than boys. Not to stereotype. But Eli would never do this.

Being compared to Eli made a small butterfly land between my shoulder blades. I tried not to notice it. Chewing up ten marshmallows seemed like creativity, but maybe it was something else. Maybe it was just a toddler's instinct to stick everything in their mouth.

Neither of us needed new shoes. We made up pretend reasons to shop. I was moving to a small town in northern Italy, and she was attending a dinner party at NBA star Jimmy Butler's house. I needed something elegant and understated; she needed to be tall enough to talk to professional basketball players. We found shoes for Italy in the men's dress aisle. That's where they put all the good leather, said Brynn. In Men's. The shoes were gray, with seams that curved like liquid eyeliner. Tiny holes patterned the sides like bouquets of baby's breath.

Brynn's boots were in Clearance. It was know-at-first-sight. They were teal. From the toe to the top of the calf, they were made of shiny rain-slickerish plastic. The heel was like a brick or a can of beans. Above the plastic there was a section of quilted snow-pant material, with a draw-string to keep it cinched over the knee. Wearing the shoes, Brynn was taller than me. Our faces were suddenly very close together. She had both hands on my shoulders to keep from falling over. The kiss, when it happened, was more like a salad than a baking project. I closed my eyes to pay attention to the separate parts as well as the whole. Here was a mouth; here was another mouth moving a little bit faster than the first mouth; here was a mouth observing and slowing down.

Brynn pulled back. So, she said, good boots?

Good boots.

We stuffed the crinkled paper back into the toes of the shoes we'd tried on. It was a way of assuaging the guilt of not purchasing them. Our love for the shoes was real, but there wasn't space for that love in real life. We said we should check for cheese samples. In the supermarket, a tower of limes greeted everyone who passed through the motion-activated doors. The limes were green and priced by the pound rather than individually. We walked up and down the aisles. Brynn had grown up eating Maria and Ricardo's tortillas, but now preferred Mission brand. There weren't any samples, of cheese or otherwise. I drove her back to her car in the center of town. When she was standing on the pavement with the car door still open, she asked if we were going to tell Eli about this.

I didn't know Eli very well. I said it was up to her.

Brynn flipped her ponytail from one shoulder to the other. She nodded. So basically, she said, this is a line, not a triangle. Thanks for the ride.

I clicked through radio stations in the empty car. One played an ad for Jan's solar company. Another didn't think we should trust the polls about the upcoming elections. Another sang a love song. What had Brynn meant about lines and triangles? It didn't matter. This not-mattering seemed to be the main difference between boys and girls. I wasn't worried about not understanding her. I wasn't sure if this meant I liked girls more than boys, or less.

•

That night, I woke up three times to pee. I woke up more than three times, but only three of the times were for peeing. Once, Athena was on my chest. She leapt away when I fluttered my eyelashes in the dark. In the bathroom I avoided the light switch. There was a moon of one shape or another—not full, not new. The shower curtain hung inky; the toilet paper glowed charcoal. I wasn't wearing underwear. Contentment was a new feeling. I could sit down all in one motion, without the interruption of pulling anything down. There was porcelain under my thighs and cotton T-shirt bunched in my armpits. These sensations felt like steps toward the future.

After the third pee, I checked my phone. It was 5:47 A.M. No notifications. Soon the sun would rise. I walked to the master bedroom and took Jan's bathrobe off the hook on the door of the walk-in closet. It was pink terry cloth and ended above my knees. I padded down the stairs and onto the porch.

The moon and sun hid behind their respective horizons. The sky was like someone had taken a dried-out eraser to black construction paper. The crickets held their breath. In the middle of the lawn stood a small skunk.

The skunk no longer looked like an adult in miniature. It had grown over the summer, and now it looked like an adult. Its fur was sleek and shiny. *Was* it an adult? Were there variables besides scale?

I stepped into the lawn. Each step felt like wading deeper, though the grass was all one length. The skunk kept its nose down, snuffing at something. Like a person treading water, it moved without moving. I stopped three yards away.

Hello, I said.

My voice tripped on the word. It was the voice of someone who hasn't spoken that day, who hasn't brushed their teeth.

The skunk froze. It lifted its tail slowly, like blowing up a balloon. I drew in a quick breath. The skunk turned and ran away.

august

In the grocery store, a stranger behind me in line said they liked my pants. I thanked them and pulled out my phone. Then I remembered the experience of being complimented was over. Ellie wasn't speaking to me. I had no one to report the small moments of my life to.

I returned my phone to my pocket and smiled again at the stranger.

They smiled back, but their lips were thinner this time.

Sorry, I said. They're new. The pants.

I faced frontward. The pants were a few years old. I'd needed an excuse. Compliments weren't supposed to mean so much; you weren't supposed to prolong eye contact with people in grocery stores.

The cart in front of me was mostly paper towels. I'd expected the large items to move quickly. The customer sorted through a big pile of coupons. Since when did people still use coupons? They handed a slip of paper to the cashier, and the cashier shook their head. Expired. A slip of paper fell to the floor and the customer bent to retrieve it. The cashier cracked their neck. Even when the right coupon was located, the customer kept their eyes lowered: hands, PIN pad, conveyor belt, wallet. These were the things that bore watching.

Finally, I unloaded a tomato, an avocado, a sleeve of tortillas, and a block of cheese from my basket. I glanced to my left. The stranger had taken their phone out. They held it in one hand, the hand resting on the push bar of their grocery cart.

Paper or plastic? said the cashier.

Oh, I said, I brought my own bag. I like your nose ring.

Thanks, they said.

Outside, the parking lot reflected sunlight back into my face. I could understand why seagulls hung around shopping malls. Previously, I'd pictured the thread between myself and my phone as a sort of tendon. Since the kiss, or since the fallout from the kiss, the thread felt more like dental floss. Nothing terrible would happen if it was cut. But this loosening wasn't happening to anyone else. I was alone with my freedom.

August was my mother's favorite month. She liked to talk about the day when she could first smell fall. She waited for it each year, and felt a shift. I'd never believed her. Cold didn't start until September. Today, though, the strap of my tote bag pressed my shirt into my armpit without making a wet spot. I turned my phone off and tucked it between the side of the bag and the sleeve of tortillas.

Ellie was making the right choice. I'd been a bad friend when I kissed Brynn, and when I didn't tell her about kissing Brynn.

Ellie had gone to the bakery. She'd been worried about her life path. Whenever she got worried about her life path, she tried to adjust her perspective. If she took enough small steps in a good direction, life would take care of itself. Chocolate was always a good direction.

She pointed to the brownie she wanted. An edge piece, not a corner. That big one, there.

Guess we're in the same boat, huh? said Eli, who was on shift that day. He slid the brownie into a wax paper bag.

Ellie liked to pay in cash. It made life more tangible, and more like a game—like Monopoly, or playing house and using leaves as money. She paused with her quarter over the tip jar.

What do you mean? she asked.

Eli, too, had eaten a brownie that morning. He, too, had been dumped.

Ellie pulled the quarter back toward her. She didn't mean to rescind the tip. She was just confused.

I wasn't—she began. I'm not—

The brownie lay on the counter between them.

Who dumped you? she asked finally. Maybe this was just one of those dumb boy things. It was a convoluted way of asking for sympathy.

Eli, by now, was realizing he'd messed up. But there was no way to backtrack, or if there was, he couldn't think of it fast enough.

Brynn, he said at last.

Ellie hadn't heard from Brynn in a couple of weeks. The romance had fizzled, she'd guessed. It wasn't a big deal—they hadn't even kissed. Still, Eli's words sent two shocks through her. The first shock was negative: Brynn and Eli had been involved. The negative part was less the information and more the fact that Ellie hadn't been privy to the information until now. The second shock was positive: Brynn had dumped Eli. Could that mean she wanted to pursue other options more seriously? Could that mean she wanted to pursue *Ellie* more seriously?

A numbness, separate from the shocks, entered Ellie's fingertips. Eli had said "too." Eli was opening and closing his mouth like a fish. There was more to the story.

I think, said Ellie, that you need to tell me everything you know.

Ellie was good at deciding what she needed, and at asking for it.

•

Brynn had dumped three people: Eli, Ellie, and me. She was moving back to Albuquerque. She'd told Eli that she would have dumped him anyway, even if she wasn't moving. She cited something about a shoe store, that he didn't understand, and something about kissing Isabel, that he did.

I took comfort in that detail. The kiss hadn't been a total waste.

The boy wasn't looking at his phone or reaching one hand into the glove box in search of the plastic fork. He was looking straight ahead and noticing the sign that said SLOW CHILDREN. It was early morning. He had many hours to drive. In another minute the trees would be orange, reflecting the light of the sun coming over the horizon. Some minutes after that, the trees would be green again. He was on his way to see a boy he wasn't dating. They had kissed before, and this evening they would kiss again. Maybe after more evenings—he tried to be reasonable, it would have to be lots and lots more evenings—they would date. The drive was nine hours. Nine was an embarrassing number of hours to drive only to kiss someone. He felt young and spontaneous at the center of this embarrassment. One hand was at ten and the other hand was at two, even though his driver's ed teacher had told him that the new rule was nine and three. His father always used to say, "What makes the children around here so slow?" when they passed those SLOW CHILDREN signs. It wasn't a funny joke. It was even less funny now than it used to be, but he still thought of it and his father probably still said it, though he hadn't seen his father for a few years now.

Have we said enough? The driver was at least as good a person as you are. The skunk stepped suddenly from the bushes and into the road.

I saw the three large birds standing at the end of Jan and Steve's driveway. I knew they were vultures right away—I was my father's daughter. *Athena, Athena,* went my heartbeat. My hands were suddenly hot on the steering wheel. The shoebox in the freezer flashed across my inner eyelids.

As I got closer, I could see my mistake. The blot on the ground was black and white, not tabby orange. The vultures lifted their heads to look at me. Since their eyes were on the sides of their heads, they stood in profile. I held off on hitting the brakes. I needed those birds to recognize my superiority—the superiority of a motor vehicle.

They didn't move. I hit the brakes. The first vulture flapped its wings once in response. All three stepped away from the carcass. They lifted off slowly, like old men standing up from their recliners.

My car came to a complete stop a few feet from the entrance to the driveway. The skunk—the body—lay exactly centered in the northbound lane. Part of it had been squished flat, but the final tuft of tail stuck up. The fur swayed slightly in a gust of wind.

Another car approached in the rearview mirror. I pulled carefully around the skunk and kept driving. At the next driveway, I turned around. Coming from this direction, Jan and Steve's was on the left. It was a wider turn. I had more space to line up the car wheels so they would pass on either side of the body.

Once I got inside, I drew the curtains. People were not like cars. We didn't mark them with models and years, or advertise updates on billboards. How, then, to remind myself that my feelings were for an Eli of the past, not an Eli who existed now? Was that even a fair distinction to make? Maybe all relationships were like that—contingent on past versions. Take Ellie, for example: if we'd met today, I couldn't have felt such deep affection for her.

I removed a cheese stick from the fridge and bit into it. Normally I ate cheese sticks in strings, peeling them off one long strand at a time. There wasn't time for that, now. A skunk had died. I took a bite without removing the plastic wrapper from the bottom of the stick.

Maybe the universe was giving me an opportunity. I could put this skunk in the ground and cover it with dirt. I could move on with my life. I took another bite of the cheese stick. It didn't seem fair. I didn't want to bury the skunk just because the universe was telling me to.

Why did the kids put beans in their ears? Because we told them no.

There was a snow shovel in the garage, and yellow rubber gloves in the cabinet beneath the sink. I picked up the shovel and put on the gloves.

The skunk didn't want to leave the pavement. I had to scrape at the edge of the carcass with the shovel to get it to unstick. The air reeked. Once it was in a trash bag, and once that trash bag was in a second trash bag, I wadded the whole thing into the shoebox. The cardboard was still cold from the freezer. It fit snugly, like a loaf of bread in a pan. I wrapped the box in two more trash bags.

Even separated by so many layers, I wondered if the smell would penetrate the rest of the freezer. Would the stored soups and blueberries be inedible? Would Jan and Steve ever speak to me again? Here, at last, was a story for my maid of honor to tell.

The black plastic looked morose among the jars of pesto. The skunk deserved better, but the shortcomings of the ceremony stemmed from material limitations, not internal ones. I felt the joy of giving something everything I had.

There were still questions. Who was the skunk in the lawn? The Eldest, in the final moments of her life? More likely it was one of her siblings. But mostly I felt settled. I didn't need to delete any phone numbers because I didn't feel the desire to click on them in the first place.

I went to Stacy's Pilates class. On the way there, I stopped at my dad's house to get a pair of leggings. I hadn't expected to need my leggings this summer. My boxes—all three of them—were stacked in one corner of the basement. Which one had the leggings in it? They all said ISABEL on the side. There was a manila file folder in the top box that was new since the last time I'd opened it.

ISABEL—DAYCARE, the label said. It was my mother's handwriting. Inside were scribbles in various colors and mediums: green crayon, red tempera paint, purple watercolor. At the back was a typed paragraph signed "Ms. Sarah."

Isabel, it said, *is a joyful and self-sufficient member of our community. She listens to directions and has an impressive attention span for someone this age. She can easily zero in on one task for an extended period of time! Because of this, she sometimes has trouble when it is time to switch from one activity to another (e.g., from art to lunch). She enjoys princesses, the swing set, and the pretend kitchen area. She plays peaceably with others. We feel so lucky to have had her in our class, and wish her the best as she moves up to the Yellow Room!*

The leggings were right underneath the file folder. I put them on in the basement so I wouldn't need to change at the studio.

Stacy grinned when I told her my plan. She set up a mat for me, right in the middle of the room, so I would have someone to follow no matter which direction we faced. I stayed at the desk, signing people in, until the last possible second.

Okay, Isabel! called Stacy when it was time. We're ready for you!

Everyone clapped.

Because I already knew about the affirmations, I'd thought of mine ahead of time: *I am trying new things.*

Though the vocabulary of the class was familiar, the movements were foreign. For donkey kicks, we were supposed to kick our legs backward, holding our knees at a ninety-degree angle. It was part of having a toned butt. It seemed simple until I looked in the mirror. My leg, unlike the other legs in the class, was not at a ninety-degree angle. My leg was at more of a sixty-degree angle. It turned out that how things felt were separate from how they looked. I couldn't trust my nerve cells to tell me where my body was, or what shape it was making.

At the top of the movement, really *squeeze* your butt, Stacy instructed. Pause for a second. The muscle won't work unless you tell it to! We create change *purposefully*!

Arms were the most painful. We moved them up and down like robots and swans and praying nuns, and then pretended to crack walnuts between our shoulder blades.

By the time we let our hands drop to our sides, bits of muscle leapt under my skin like toads under a bedsheet. I couldn't predict when or where the toads were going to jump.

After class, Stacy asked me if I'd liked it.

No, don't answer that, she said. Wait a few days. Your body will feel different tomorrow, and different again the next day. On the third day, you can decide if you like Pilates or not.

Ellie asked if I could come over.

When I got there, one of her roommates, Fern, was making kimchi. Shards of cabbage littered the kitchen. They were working from a video recipe. They kept having to dry the salt water from their hands to scroll back and rewatch sections.

Here, I texted Ellie. I let myself in through the screen door.

What have you been up to these days? Fern asked. I'd met them before, when I'd been home on break from college, though their hair was a different color than the last time I'd visited. Ellie and Fern had lived together for years.

I figured we'd be seeing a ton of you this summer, they said. But I guess our paths haven't crossed.

I'm a receptionist at a yoga studio, I said, studying the mounds of vegetables on the cutting board. I babysit. I've been house-sitting, but I need to find a new place for September. I don't know. Did you grow these peppers yourself?

Fern put down their knife. Oh, they said, well—

They broke off, frowning. Oh. Never mind.

What?

They shook their head. I forget what I was going to say. Yes, I grew the peppers.

I nodded. The knife thumped against the wood and we didn't have to speak.

Ellie came out of her room. She waltzed to the cutting board and stole a piece of carrot without asking.

Porch, she said, pointing back outside.

To call Ellie's porch a "porch" was generous. It was a stoop made of wood. We sat on the steps.

I'm sorry, I said, once we were sitting down.

Ellie sighed. She hugged her knees into her chest and picked at a hangnail on her big toe. She believed I was sorry, but she didn't believe I wouldn't do it all again.

I had really hurt her feelings when I kissed Brynn and didn't tell her about it, she said. Or when Brynn had kissed me. The kiss wasn't even what hurt—it was finding out about it from *Eli*, of all people. It didn't matter. That wasn't what she wanted to talk about. She had something she needed to tell me, that she should have told me before. So maybe she understood now—how hard it could be to tell people the things they deserved to know.

The mail truck trundled by. It paused at Ellie's mailbox, then grumbled onward without dropping anything off. We both waved at the driver.

I'm moving, Ellie said. She looked sideways at me, then back at her toes.

Maybe not forever, maybe just for the fall. But I leave this weekend.

Ellie had gotten a job at a state forest in Vermont. She would lead nature walks for families. She would point out red efts, and places where lightning had struck trees. When it rained, there would be educational materials to design: brochures and scavenger hunts and water cycle coloring pages. The forest called it a "fellowship" because it was just for the fall, but there were opportunities for advancement. Her friend, the one she had visited earlier in the summer, had a spare room.

I pictured Ellie in thick hiking boots, with a backpack covered in drawstrings. She looked happy. I couldn't decide where the happiness came from. Was it the draw-strings, or the fact that she was Ellie?

That's wonderful, I told her.

She looked at one of my eyes, and then the other. I'm really excited, she said.

I'm happy for you.

You don't mind? That I'll be gone?

I said obviously I would miss her, but we weren't attached. She wasn't responsible for me. I knew other people in this town.

I didn't say that she hadn't been speaking to me, anyway.

And you'll have to visit, she said.

Did this mean I'd been forgiven? I stretched out my feet beyond the steps, into the lawn. The news came to rest inside my belly as a relief. We knew how to do long distance. We were good at it. With Ellie in Vermont, our friendship could continue.

Did you like it? she asked after a moment.

Like what?

Kissing a girl.

She'd turned toward me, and was leaning back against the railing. Yes, I was forgiven. It seemed important to answer honestly, as a way of saying "thank you." I thought about which words to pick.

Yes, I said. I liked it. But does that mean anything? Like, isn't kissing like a massage? It feels nice, objectively. No matter who's doing it, or if there's "chemistry" or whatever.

I did the air quotes with my fingers.

And was there chemistry?

I don't know!

Ellie sighed. Her hair was still damp from the shower. The pieces at her temples had dried in fluffy ringlets, framing her face. I wondered, not for the first time, if Ellie was the person I should be kissing. I didn't think so. But hadn't Pilates shown me how skewed my self-perception was? Why did people kiss, in the first place? It always seemed a bit desperate—as if the kissers needed some physical proof of how close they felt in that moment, or were worried they would never feel so close again. On the steps with Ellie, I didn't fear the future. There had been times in our friendship when we'd been closer than we were right then, and there would be times in the future that we'd be closer still. We didn't need to kiss.

Anyway, said Ellie. You can sublet my room, if you want. Fern would be happy if it was you.

Oh! I said. Oh. I mean. How much is the rent?

The offer seemed like more than I deserved. I said I would think about it. My friendship with Ellie would survive, even if the planet didn't. Relational history was hard to outweigh, which was one of its benefits as well as its curses. You could mess up pretty majorly and still be a net positive in someone's life.

By now it was midmorning. We stayed on the steps, watching the sun drag itself up the ladder of the sky. Maybe the sun, too, was a small child preparing to brave the playground's tallest slide. We said it out loud—that we hadn't seen each other as much as we expected to this summer, even before all the Brynn drama. Ellie couldn't picture a day in the recent life of Isabel. What time did I wake up? What did I eat for breakfast? What did I think about? She didn't like not being able to picture me.

I asked for the address of her place in Vermont, and she texted it to me right then so I would have it in my phone. I said I would write her a letter, with a stamp and everything. I would try to explain.

There was a moment when the Middle Skunk and the Third Skunk were bereft. The Middle Skunk was the oldest, and no longer in the middle of anything. The Third Skunk was one of two. Their titles didn't fit. But the skunks had always been pieces of a whole. It had always been a coincidence that they were three, instead of two, or a billion. Whatever had belonged to the Eldest Skunk came to rest in her siblings. Their taste buds held a memory of rust and squash blossom that hadn't been there before.

The skunks ate worms from the fruit that fell out of the apple tree. It was getting colder at night, and they slept under the porch instead of under the forsythia. In the morning they were quiet. Why did they keep dreaming about pigs and goats? Neither of them had ever seen a pig, or a goat. It didn't make sense.

The Third Skunk helped the Middle Skunk lick the patch of fur behind her ear. The wind blew.

It was time to harvest the potatoes. The plants had died back early this year. Once the stems and leaves were brown, my father prepared to dig for the roots. I'd helped every autumn when I was small, but never while I was in college.

We took turns with the spade. When my father stomped the blade into the earth, it was a continuation of his leg. He pried the handle back like an oar through water. He canoed; he danced; he did his job. The dirt flipped over. I crouched on the other side of the bed. I watched for the circles of gold and pried them out with my fingers. With the first turn, the soil moved in large bricks, still stuck together. After I pulled the obvious potatoes, we did a second pass. The dirt crumbled in my fists like a block of feta cheese. My dad prodded through with the tip of the spade. Any clod large enough to hide a root vegetable had to be deconstructed.

At each fresh stomp of the spade, we held our breath. There was always the chance that the shovel would hit a potato, splitting it in two before its time. Sometimes there was a noise when it happened—something like a bite from an apple. I watched my father's face as he stomped. Even if a potato's death was silent, you could see it in his eyes. He could feel when he'd hit something.

The crescents at the tops of my fingernails turned black. I sat back on my heels and wiped sweat from my eyebrow. Dirt clung to my pores in its wake. It felt sort of like the clay masks you could buy in the skin care aisle.

When it was my turn with the spade, I struggled. The top of the metal cut painfully into the sole of my foot, even through the garden clogs I'd borrowed from Brigitte, and the earth never moved in one piece. I had to tug at the handle multiple times to convince it to shift. Still, I kept at it. My father sorted through the clumps of dirt. Elegance didn't matter—we would find the potatoes either way.

He told me about a deer he'd seen last week. He'd been driving home at night from a potluck. The deer had been in the road. Seeing deer like this always left him shaken. If you hit one and it went through the windshield, you were both goners. At the same time, the deer was beautiful. My father couldn't help but feel grateful for the encounter.

He pulled a long thin potato from the ground. Humph, he said. Thinks it's a sweet potato, does it!

He put it in the basket.

What about you? he asked. Any wildlife sightings?

"Any wildlife sightings?" was our stock question. It was what I'd asked, over the phone, when I was at college and wanted to hear his voice. If I paid attention to the answer was beside the point. He would talk about the red foxes. His voice would keep going. For him, maybe it really was about the animals. In the city I'd never had much to report—a Great Dane in rain boots, but that was different.

There was a skunk, again, I said. I wiggled the spade farther into the earth.

It almost sprayed me. It lifted its tail and everything. For a second I was so sure—but then nothing. It was almost disappointing.

My father nodded. Maybe it's genetic, he said.

What?

Oh, come on. I've told you my skunk story before, haven't I?

I let go of the spade and rubbed at the dirt on my forehead. My father had many stories. If one of them was about a skunk, surely I would have remembered it by now. This summer, of all summers, something would have reminded me.

My father dusted off a potato. He cleared his throat.

As he spoke, it came back to me. In the story, he's camping. The heat's unbearable, so he drags his sleeping bag outside the tent in search of a cross breeze. He wakes in the middle of the night with the weight of a small mammal on his chest. He blinks at the skunk. It whips around, tail in the air. And then it's gone. It runs away.

So you see, said my dad, it must be genetic. These skunks getting ready to spray us, and then chickening out.

I folded my hands on top of the spade. Do you think it means they like us more, or less?

My dad laughed. Next time, he said, ask the skunk.

I looked it up later, on my phone. Skunks were twenty times better at smelling than humans, it turned out. They weren't immune to themselves. Especially when close to home, they tried not to spray if they could help it.

We laid the potatoes in lines on the grass and hosed them off. My dad sorted them into piles: soup potatoes, baking potatoes, use-up-fast-before-they-rot potatoes. After they dried, we weighed them pile by pile to calculate the total crop.

Three pounds more than last year, my dad said proudly. Good work, Isabel.

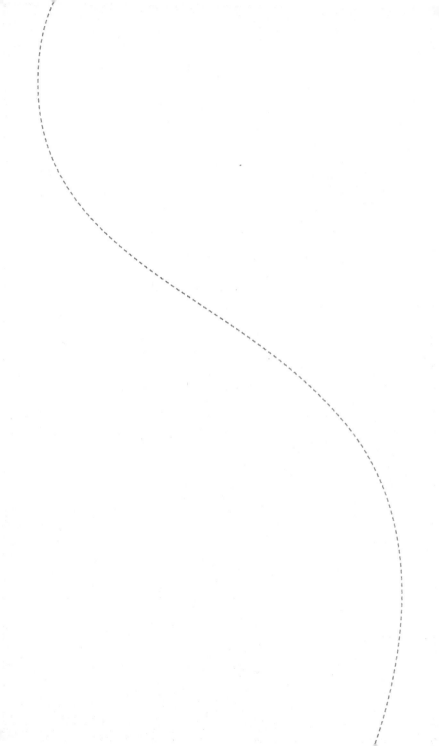

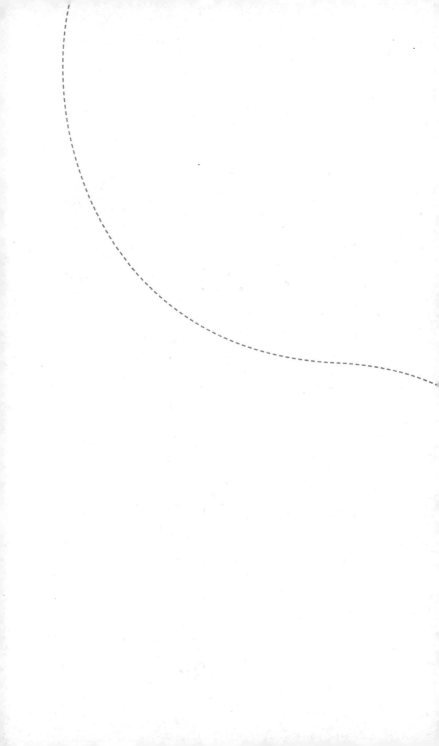

acknowledgments

The Skunks owes particular thanks to:

My agent Elizabeth, my editor Masie, designer Beth, and everyone at Tin House—for turning this story from a file on my computer into a beautiful, printed, shareable thing.

Allegra, Emily, Anna, David, Josh, Stiliana, and Lynn—my wise and enthusiastic professors.

Dada—the source of all floral and faunal knowledge.

Nick—my friend, my reader, my oracle!

Erin, Janelle, and Sam—you keep me sane.

Fiona Warnick grew up in Western Massachusetts and holds a BA in creative writing from Oberlin College, where she won the Emma Howell Poetry Prize. She teaches preschool in Providence, Rhode Island.